"I thought you'd be driving a Mercedes,"

Doug said with a smirk as they got to her sleek gray convertible. "And every single one of those pearls around your neck was once on intimate terms with an oyster, eh?"

"I repeat, Doug Stewart," and Laurel slammed the door for punctuation, "you are the worst snob I have ever known. The way you see things, the world is divided up into the evil rich and the noble poor, right? A lot you know."

Doug groaned as though mortally wounded. "I only know one thing. I want you and I'm going to have you, and it's going to be on my turf and my terms, do you understand me?" His arms went around her as his lips took complete possession of hers, burning her mouth with the heat of his desire, forcing open the gates to her body and soul.

Dear Reader:

As the months go by, we continue to receive word from you that SECOND CHANCE AT LOVE romances are providing you with the kind of romantic entertainment you're looking for. In your letters you've voiced enthusiastic support for SECOND CHANCE AT LOVE, you've shared your thoughts on how personally meaningful the books are, and you've suggested ideas and changes for future books. Although we can't always reply to your letters as quickly as we'd like, please be assured that we appreciate your comments. Your thoughts are all-important to us!

We're glad many of you have come to associate SECOND CHANCE AT LOVE books with our butterfly trademark. We think the butterfly is a perfect symbol of the reaffirmation of life and thrilling new love that SECOND CHANCE AT LOVE heroines and heroes find together in each story. We hope you keep asking for the "butterfly books," and that, when you buy one—whether by a favorite author or a talented new writer—you're sure of a good read. You can trust all SECOND CHANCE AT LOVE books to live up to the high standards of romantic fiction you've come to expect.

So happy reading, and keep your letters coming!

With warm wishes,

Ellen Edwards

Ellen Edwards
SECOND CHANCE AT LOVE
The Berkley/Jove Publishing Group
200 Madison Avenue
New York, NY 10016

Second Chance at Love™

TWILIGHT EMBRACE
JENNIFER ROSE

SECOND CHANCE AT LOVE
BOOK

TWILIGHT EMBRACE

First edition published November 1982

First printing

"Second Chance at Love" and the butterfly emblem are trademarks belonging to Jove Publications, Inc.

Printed in the United States of America

Second Chance at Love books are published by
The Berkley/Jove Publishing Group
200 Madison Avenue, New York, NY 10016

To Caroline and Saul,
Class A players on and off the fairways

TWILIGHT EMBRACE

chapter

1

THE TALL, RUGGED-LOOKING man on the practice tee took a bright-orange golf ball out of a canvas bag, teed it up, gripped his driver, and settled into a wide stance. Broad shoulders moved fluidly in a ninety-degree turn as he drew his club back and up, bracing against his right leg at the top of his backswing.

Laurel Campion shook her blond head in disbelief as she watched the man from her vantage point on the grassy rise between the clubhouse and the practice tee. She'd been taught that a golfer's swing was as individual as a thumbprint, but there, in front of her eyes, a perfect stranger was wielding his club exactly as she'd seen Reed Campion wield his club hundreds of times. Her slender body arched knowingly as the stranger connected with the ball, sending it streaking across the placid blue of the

1

Connecticut early-morning summer sky, before he brought his driver around and up over his left shoulder—in a startling replica of Reed Campion's high finish.

Who is he? How dare he? Indignant questions flashed across Laurel's mind as she watched the stranger take another practice ball out of his bag and tee it up. Even the way he bent deeply at the knee when he teed up— as if he were about to dance the limbo—painfully reminded her of Reed.

Trying to break the stranger's mesmerizing hold on her, Laurel quickly forced herself to catalog the differences between the two men. Reed's hair had been silvery and sleekly cut; the stranger's hair was the color of a warm beach and grazed his collar. Reed had been six feet tall and slim, with an elegant build like Fred Astaire; the stranger was two inches taller and—a word springing unbidden to Laurel's mind—*flagrantly* muscular. Now that she was actively taking the man's measure, nearly everything about him struck her as flagrant—from the new orange golf balls, which Reed would have spurned in favor of traditional white, to a swaggering air of self-confidence that wafted toward Laurel on the morning breeze. Even his faded jeans seemed a loud announcement, the sort of proclamation made by club members' teenage children who wanted to flaunt their rebelliousness at the same time that they happily charged the latest stainless-steel putters to their parents' accounts.

The stranger was no teenager, though. He looked to be in his late thirties, three or four years older than Laurel... and years younger than she'd ever known Reed, except in photos. Was he a new club member, Laurel wondered, as her cool blue eyes took in both the canvas bag of balls at the man's feet and the caddy out on the practice fairway, shagging the balls as they landed near the three-hundred-yard marker. A member would have been hitting old balls from one of the pro shop's wire buckets. The sandy-haired man could only be one

of the touring pros who would be playing in the Southern
New England Classic, scheduled to start in two hours.

Laurel's heart quickened. As the women's champion
of Falling Water Country Club, she'd agreed to play in
the pro-amateur eighteen-hole best-ball round that would
precede the three days of fiercely competitive professional play. She'd worked on her game that winter in
Boca Raton, Florida, with Ronnie Pulane, her favorite
teaching pro, and she'd brushed up on her putting these
last two weeks with Buzz Newfield, the venerable Falling
Water pro. She'd been confident of doing herself and the
club proud—until she'd seen the disturbing stranger on
the practice tee whose swing hauntingly evoked her dead
husband and chipped away at her famous control.

If only Reed could come back to life and be there
with her! He would be so pleased that Falling Water was
host, for the first time, to a Professional Golf Association
Tour event. He would have fought at Laurel's side against
the club diehards, including Reed's own brother, Evan,
and sister-in-law, Sara, who'd bitterly opposed the coming of the Classic on the theory that it would bring a
certain "element" onto the sacred club grounds. And how
excited Reed would be that Laurel was playing in the
pro-am round, the only woman in the field. It had been
Reed who had first put a golf club in Laurel's hands,
declared that she was a natural, and insisted that she take
lessons to make the most of her gift.

Suddenly Laurel panicked. Without Reed to cheer her
on, would she be able to play even a semblance of her
best game? She had horrible visions of dribbling the ball
off the first tee as the onlookers blushed in embarrassment
for her... landing in the fiendish sand trap on the third
hole and in the famous water on the twelfth... four-
putting the eighteenth green as the sportscaster from the
Hartford televison station narrated her agony. Damn the
stranger on the practice tee for destroying her equilibrium!

"Laurel, my darling, you look as though you've seen a ghost," a throaty voice said in a wry drawl.

Laurel turned in relief as Elsie Howard hailed her. The tall, lithe, fair Laurel and the rounder, dark-haired Elsie were known around Falling Water as the Bobbsey Twins, because neither their physical dissimilarity nor the fourteen-point difference in their handicaps stood in the way of sisterly closeness. "Oh, Elsie, I think I have seen a ghost." Laurel pointed toward the muscular sandy-haired stranger. "Is that a reincarnation of Reed's swing, or is it?"

Elsie watched the stranger belt the ball down the practice fairway, then waved her hand dismissively. "Good grief," she said, borrowing, as she often did, from her eight-year-old twins' vocabulary. "You're just worked up because of the tournament. Let's go down and hit off a bucket. You'll feel much better."

"I can't go to the practice tee as long as he's there," Laurel wailed.

"You're not going to tell me you got me up at the crack of dawn just to talk! I've got to get into that skinny little nothing dress Pete bought me in London—in about ten hours," Elsie added, consulting her watch. "I need some exercise. And you need to unwind. Come on."

Laurel stubbornly stood her ground. "The whole idea of getting here so early was because I thought we'd have the practice tee to ourselves."

"Laurel, what's the matter with you? You're not really jittery, are you? When I think of you sinking that thirty-foot putt on the eighteenth during the Connecticut Women's Amateur, in front of that huge gallery, and the awful heat—" A breeze riffled through Elsie's dark hair, and she brushed back her thick bangs. "You can do anything, and you know it. Just remember—Campion rhymes with champion. And you look gorgeous, by the way, which never hurts. Love that blue skirt and hair band. No wind is going to get underneath *that* hair band.

Next to you, Princess Grace looks messy."

"Thanks—I think," Laurel said. Elsie was always telling her that she should "unbend" her looks—wear shorts to show off her long slim legs, wear her shoulder-length blond hair in a fashionable tangle instead of the pageboy she favored. But Reed had liked classic looks, and Laurel still used his standards as her guide. "I just wish Reed were here," she said mournfully.

"Of course you do, darling. But he's not, and there's nothing you can do about it, and the last thing he'd want would be for you to stand around playing the weepy widow. If you want to honor Reed Campion, you'll get out there today and hit the hooey out of that ball."

Laurel burst into laughter. "Hit the *hooey* out of it?"

"All right, the hell out of it," she chuckled. "For the Gipper and all that. Now, are we going to hit off a bucket or stand here forever?"

Below them on the practice tee the sandy-haired stranger put his driver back into his bag and took out an iron.

"Pretty determined, whoever he is," Elsie said, as the two women started down the grassy rise. "He must be one of the rabbits—you know, one of the newcomers on the PGA tour."

Laurel didn't respond. She knew they would have to pass by the practice tee to get to the pro shop, and for no reason that she could fathom, the thought of being near the stranger filled her with a tension not unlike the oddly exciting fear she sometimes experienced when she was driving her Mercedes convertible alone at night over deserted country roads.

She directed her thoughts to the rolling green lushness of her surroundings. Her husband had liked to say that women looked best in the evening, but golf courses looked best in the morning, and she shared the sentiment. The dew was still sparkling on the manicured reaches of the first fairway, off to her right. The darker grass of the first green was hidden around a dogleg turn, but she could see it in her mind's eye, could almost feel its cushiony planes beneath her cleated white shoes. At this early point in the day, even the sand traps looked good— neatly raked, and unmarred by careless footprints. Her anxiety forgotten, Laurel felt hopeful anticipation now, as she thought about sending a ball down the first fairway. Playing golf on your home course was like making love within a great marriage—always new. She had her reservations about the Falling Water Country Club and country-club life in general, but she adored the course itself—as she'd adored the husband she'd lost two years earlier when he was fifty, after too brief a marriage.

Laurel steeled herself as she and Elsie neared the practice tee. She was close enough to the stranger to see the weathered cast to his complexion, the dramatic eyebrows glinting red in the sunlight, and a jaw that all but vibrated with determination. Hardly a conventionally handsome face, yet an indisputably arresting one—the face of an outlaw-turned-hero in a western movie, or maybe a hero-turned-outlaw. Laurel felt an urgent need to move out of their shared space before she found out which one he was, but he looked up at the two women, seemed about to dismiss them from his mind, then unaccountably locked eyes with Laurel, virtually pinioning her with his gaze. Laurel sensed her shoulders, her elbows, the backs of her knees growing hot; her whole body was suddenly patchy with heat. His lips curled in a sneer and the man widened his hazel eyes, making Laurel feel as though her very soul were being X-rayed. Abruptly he gave a knowing little nod and turned his attention back to the five iron in his hand. Gasping, stumbling, Laurel moved on.

"Laurel?" Elsie said, concern bringing her voice several notches above its usual throaty alto.

"Did you see the way that man looked at me? You did, didn't you?" Laurel's own cool voice was tremulous.

"Don't try telling me I'm just having tournament jitters. If that wasn't the very definition of undressing someone with your eyes, I don't know what is!"

"Are you talking about the way he looked at you or the way *you* looked at *him,* darling?" Elsie asked.

"What?" Laurel stopped dead still. Her heart felt as if it were trying to escape through her chest wall.

"Don't give me 'what,' darling. That man attracted the hooey out of you. Sorry—the hell out of you, and it's about time somebody did. You haven't looked this animated in two years." Then she added, "Don't quote me to Pete, but I wish the man had done a little of that eye work on me. Devilishly appealing."

"Elsie, don't be absurd. You know what touring pros are like. Low scorers on the course, big scorers off. Oh, I wish I'd never agreed to play in this damn event."

Several high-school boys who caddied during the summer came out of the pro shop and waved at Laurel and Elsie.

"Good luck, Mrs. Campion," a thin, dark-haired boy said.

"Thanks, Donald." She almost added that she wished he were carrying her bag that day, but she didn't want to be disloyal to her stepson, Dean, who'd asked to caddy for her so he could be a part of the excitement of the Classic. Considering Dean's behavior so far that summer, Laurel was less than certain that he'd manage to peel himself out of bed to get to the first tee for her nine-fifty starting time. And, like the infuriating man at the practice tee, Dean would no doubt manage to produce his grubbiest jeans to thumb his nose at the grandees of Falling Water. Laurel noted approvingly that Donald was wearing immaculate, pressed khakis and a brand-new striped two-button shirt, and complimented him on his appearance.

"Gee, thanks, Mrs. Campion," he said. "Not like your rabbit, right? But if I could hit a ball like that, I guess I wouldn't care what I wore, either."

"My rabbit?" Laurel echoed. Her foursome for the pro-am round included an unknown Toronto pro named Doug Stewart, and two Falling Water duffers who were on the board of directors of Inner City Youth, the local charity that would receive the profits from the Southern New England Classic. Even as she asked the question, she steadied herself for the inevitable answer.

"Sure," Donald said. "Didn't you know that was Doug Stewart down there on the practice tee? I bet you're really looking forward to going eighteen holes with him!"

chapter

2

LINGERING IN THE pro shop to buy a new package of golf balls and to chat with club pro Buzz Newfield, Laurel managed to use up nearly half an hour before she and Elsie got back to the practice tee. To Laurel's relief, the maddening Doug Stewart had vanished. But as she teed up a ball she realized he might as well have still been there, so strong was the impression he'd made on her. It wasn't his unconventional good looks or even the uncanny way his swing resembled Reed's that dominated her thoughts: what had gotten to her was his taking all of ten seconds to look her over, then broadcasting the unmistakable message "I've got your number." Little did he know, Laurel mused.

Orphaned at five when her parents died in an automobile accident, Laurel had grown up with her Aunt Bett and Uncle Jack and their children in Windsor, an historic but economically underpowered town to the north of Hartford, in Connecticut's Tobacco Valley. She'd been treated with kindness, but she'd always felt like an outsider, a flower transplanted into foreign soil, doomed to be regarded as a weed because its beauty wasn't recognized. She put herself through Farmingdale College, only fifteen miles to the west of Hartford, but in its moneyed, New England pristineness a thousand miles from Windsor, and she'd found herself odd woman out again. Instead of wondering what color Fiat she should demand for her eighteenth birthday, she was frantically worrying about how to carry two waitressing jobs, do all her course work, *and* occasionally sleep. By the time she'd gone to work as a financial analyst for Nutmeg State Life Insurance in Hartford, she'd almost believed in the image she'd defensively created for herself—that of a cool, even aloof, woman who never doubted her own judgment or surrendered control over a situation.

When she'd married Reed Campion, president of the insurance conglomerate, she'd believed she was signing on for a lifetime run in her invented role. Reed had found her ice-maiden persona endlessly exciting and had installed her in the perfect ice palace—an imposing white colonnaded early nineteenth-century house in Farmingdale, not far from the college where Laurel had once struggled to make ends meet. Because she had loved Reed and felt grateful to him, she had never disturbed his pleasure in her by forcing him to look beneath her surface and to see her molten core. Besides, the cool mask helped convince Reed's friends that the much-younger Laurel was their emotional contemporary . . . and had convinced Laurel herself that she was a grown-up among grown-ups. Doug Stewart, however, had seen her molten core, her girlish heart. They hadn't exchanged so much as a word, yet his penetrating hazel eyes had bored through the protective layers of frost to the part of Laurel where fantasies ran rampant and sensuality knew no bounds, where playfulness mattered more than winning. He'd seen the *real* Laurel—or had he? As her blue eyes followed the trajectory of her practice ball, she wondered if years of role playing hadn't perhaps altered her very nature. Maybe the coolness was her reality now, the molten core a cherished illusion. Regardless of which Laurel was the real one, she knew for certain which Laurel *she* was comfortable being—and that was the unruffled persona she'd invented long ago and perfected over the course of time. Doug Stewart had to be regarded as an enemy, almost a blackmailer, someone who knew a dreadful secret about her which she had to keep concealed at any cost.

"Drat the cat!" Elsie interrupted Laurel's reverie. "I just broke the zipper on my skirt." She turned around, and Laurel saw the revealing gap. "Cottage cheese and water for me all week," Elsie vowed penitently, not for the first time.

"Maybe it's just that you've finally started swinging at the ball," Laurel said. "That left wrist was looking good and firm."

"Oh, darling, why do you even bother to look at my swing? I'm about as likely to become a Class A golfer as you are to become a go-go dancer." Elsie put her driver in her golf bag. "I've got to go up to the clubhouse and change. Don't want your gallery to disgrace you. Meet me in the grillroom? I could do with some coffee. Black."

"All right," Laurel agreed. "I'll hit off the rest of the bucket, then join you."

For the next few minutes, Laurel banished all extraneous thoughts from her mind and concentrated on becoming one with the golf club. She focused with almost trancelike intensity on the sweet spot, the point on the striking surface of the club that ideally met the ball each time a shot was played. *There*. And there. And there.

Her spirits soared as she sent three perfect drives out into space.

"And you didn't even muss your hair," a deep voice commented behind her.

Laurel whirled. Doug Stewart was standing there, his mouth arranged in a one-sided curve that managed to be leer, sneer, and grin all at once.

"Unlike you," Laurel snapped, "I've outgrown adolescence and no longer regard unkempt hair as a sign of spiritual superiority."

"Well, well, well. What a pretty little speech." The muscular golf pro clapped his hands with mocking slowness. "The good Lord has seen fit to bless you with a pack of unruly teenagers to practice your delivery on? Except that you're too young to have teenage kids—even if you *are* wearing a skirt that should be illegal to sell to anyone under fifty."

Laurel looked at Doug Stewart's expectant face and gave silent thanks that her mastery over herself extended to her capillaries—there would be no telltale flush in *her* cheeks. She narrowed her eyes. "You're rude," she said, turning to tee up another ball.

"Rude," he agreed, forcing himself into her field of vision, "and crude, and just your kind of golfer, eh?" His deep voice had a lilt, which Laurel recognized as English Canadian; his words were all his own. "I like that compact swing of yours. Very controlled, like everything else about you, Lady Blue. I love your hand work. In fact, let's go somewhere and talk about your hand work. Then again," he eyed her wickedly, "the hell with talking—let's go somewhere and do something with it."

The man knew secrets of hers—and she knew a thing or two about him. He was just waiting for a snappy put-down, and Laurel decided to deny him the pleasure of battle, though a dozen sharp retorts rose to her lips. She drew her club back as if she had nothing on her mind but golf and sent the ball on the same true flight as its three predecessors. Belying her calm surface, her emotions chugged, her mind raced. There was no way she could play eighteen holes with Doug Stewart in the pressure cooker of a big event. Maybe there was still time to get herself into a different foursome, or out of the event altogether—but how? She couldn't let Falling Water down. She couldn't let Reed down. And she wouldn't give her sister-in-law, Sara, the satisfaction of knowing that a certain "element" among the touring pros had flapped the unflappable Laurel Campion.

"Do you have a name, Lady Blue?" he asked. Then, without waiting for an answer, "Mine is Doug Stewart. You never heard of me, but you will—everyone will. This is my first tour event, and I'm planning to win it. You like winners? Then I'm yours until nine-fifty." He put a hand on her driver, as though to take it away, and her knees felt suddenly unreliable, as though he were touching some intimate part of her body. "How about showing me the back nine?" he went on brashly. "Won't be anyone else out there at this hour. We'll find some properly contoured green. There's nothing like making love on the green on a summer day." His banter suddenly stopped. "My God, you're beautiful. I don't think I can wait another minute. Let's do it right here. Anyone who comes down to practice can just tee up on our fannies." His mouth relaxed in a genuine smile.

Laurel couldn't check her own smile. She had a ludicrous, wonderful image of haughty Sara Campion coming down to hit off a few shots and finding Laurel writhing on the ground in a passionate embrace with a long-haired stranger. Laurel squelched her smile, but too late. Doug Stewart had seen it for the assent it was. He was moving in on her, his powerful, tanned arms going around her, his lips meeting hers in a searing, demanding kiss. The long-banked fires at Laurel's center burst into flame as her lips were forced open and her mouth was invaded. Her driver thudded unheeded to the ground, her hands went to Doug's back, pulling at him as he was pulling at her, until her hungry breasts found relief against the broad contours of his chest.

It was Doug who broke the torrid embrace, holding Laurel at arm's length, shaking his head as his piercing gaze traveled her face. "Lady Blue," he said huskily, "I suppose it's too much to hope for that you're happily divorced?"

His words were like a bucket of cold water flung on her flames. shortly before the accident that had claimed his life, Reed had told her, in a moment of eerie precognition, that if he died before she did, she had to marry again, be happy again. But he'd never instructed her to insult his memory by grappling with an arrogant stranger within view of the pro shop and anyone who might pass by.

"It is too much to hope for, Mr. Stewart," Laurel said stiffly. She peeled the pale blue golfer's glove off her left hand, revealing a thin gold band. "Good luck with the tournament," she added formally, walking away. She would stick her head in the doorway at the pro shop to tell them she'd finished practicing, then she'd join Elsie in the grillroom for a much-needed cold drink.

Doug's strong right hand caught her around the waist. "Hold on, Lady Blue. You don't think you can just dismiss me that way, do you?"

"I'm late to meet someone," Laurel said through clenched teeth, trying ineffectually to pry his fingers loose.

"What do you think I am—your caddy?" Doug's mouth was a sneer again. "Off to the grillroom, are you, to have a cup of tea with one of the privileged few? I bet you drink your tea with your pinky finger curled. You're a snob, Lady Blue, and, what's worse, you're a liar."

"A liar?"

"You're already telling yourself that I stole those

kisses from you, but you gave them willingly. Gave them gratefully I would say—if I weren't a gentleman."

"Some gentleman," Laurel taunted, batting at the hand that still gripped her waist.

"Careful there," Doug said. "Don't hurt my million-dollar fingers." He let her go, but with a look underscoring the innuendo in his words. "See you in my gallery? I'm going to win the Classic for your favor, Lady Blue. Just like Robin Hood, who did it all just to get a kiss from Maid Marion. Only I'll expect more than a kiss when I get through robbing the rich—a lot more."

His words ringing in her ears, his touch lingering on her fevered body, Laurel hurried toward the sanctuary of the clubhouse.

In sharp contrast with the dewy, virginal look of the golf course, the rest of the club grounds looked more and more like a carnival midway. As Laurel hurried away from the practice tee, she had second thoughts. Maybe Evan and Sara Campion had been right in their opposition to holding the Classic at Falling Water. She scanned the volunteer marshals setting up an admissions area with stanchions and ropes, the concessionaires expertly erecting gaudy striped tents, where food and drink would be sold to thousands of people over the next four days. Even now the parking lot was starting to fill up with a public eager to cheer on their favorites among the great and famous touring golf pros . . . or perhaps to root for an unknown, a rabbit, dreaming of snatching the sixty-thousand-dollar winner's purse and instant elevation to athletic stardom.

Laurel's stomach contracted as she caught the smell of hot dogs grilling in one of the tents. Hot dogs at eight-thirty in the morning! But as she watched a group of men hoist a bright-yellow silken pennant with large purple felt letters, she remembered what the next four days were really about, and her qualms vanished. Inner City Youth and Falling Water Country Club Welcome You to the Southern New England Classic, the pennant declared. Reed had been active on the board of ICY, a charity that funded a wide variety of sports programs for under-privileged Hartford area children, including a coed summer camp on nearby Avon Mountain, where Laurel's favorite caddy, Donald Gibson, had first been introduced to golf. The difference between the gate receipts and the winning pros' purses would go to ICY. And the gate receipts were swelled considerably by the three hundred celebrities and other amateurs who, like Laurel, had paid two thousand dollars apiece for the privilege of playing in the opening day best-ball round.

No way, she decided fiercely, was she going to let some aggressive, cocky upstart scare her off from this very special event *or* undermine her ability to play. Her normal sense of purpose and self-assuredness coursed through her veins as she entered the cool white two-storied clubhouse. Architecturally on par with her own home and the other black-shuttered white houses of Main Street in Farmingdale, the building always gave her a conscious sensation of well-being. Its understated New England elegance was such a far cry from Aunt Bett and Uncle Jack's hopelessly jumbled brick house. "I belong here," she told herself with a ferocious intensity. But another interior voice, a mocking voice, told her that if she really belonged, she wouldn't have to keep reminding herself of the fact.

She paused outside the grillroom, as she always did, in front of the bank of photographs of past club presidents. There, at the end of the line, was Reed Campion, masterful and distinguished even in the banal formality of the corporate-style portrait. Damn, oh damn, why had fate been so cruel to him, just when he had everything he wanted? The presidency of Nutmeg State Life Insurance . . . the presidency of Falling Water . . . and a loving Laurel to fill the void left by his first wife, Eleanor, who'd deserted Reed and infant Dean to live in the south of France and indulge her artistic ambitions.

Suppressing a sigh, Laurel waved at lanky, gray-haired Webb Daniels, Reed's lawyer and a perennial bachelor who had been courting her in his own low-keyed style. Over the past year they had gone to the Civic Center in downtown Hartford for hockey games, to the Tanglewood summer music festival in the nearby Berk-shire Mountains for open-air Beethoven, and to the club on Saturday nights for dinner and a few sedate turns around the dance floor.

"You can't bring him back, Laurel," Webb commented gently, as she stole another look at the photograph of Reed.

"I know. But I'm allowed to reminisce a little, aren't I?"

"No statute on the books against reminiscing," Webb said. "But you don't want to go making a profession of it, either." He put a hand on Laurel's shoulder. "You know your problem? You've never cried over Reed. You didn't cry at his funeral, and I'd bet my new MacGregor woods that you haven't cried since. That's what you need, old girl—one big flood of tears. Then maybe you can let him go and get on with living your life."

"Wait a minute," Laurel objected lightly. "I cried all over you at that Hartford Stage Company production of *Damn Yankees.*"

"Sure," Webb agreed. "Easy tears. I'm talking about an absolute storm, a cataclysm, from way down deep inside you where the pain is."

"Why, Webb, I never thought of you as the primal-scream type. Letting it all hang out and that kind of nonsense." She eyed his gray cable-knit Shetland sweater, cuffed khakis, and brown Bass Weejun moccasins, the timeless weekend uniform of the the New England male—moderate and neutral in most things, including emotion. "You're beginning to sound like Dean," she sighed, invoking the seventeen-year-old stepson whose indulgent, undisciplined ways had lately been a major source of concern to her.

"Heaven forbid," Webb murmured. "I love Dean, but I can't say I like him lately. He must be quite a handful for you on your own." He gave a little laugh, then squeezed Laurel's shoulder before dropping his hand. "What am I doing, creating such heavy weather on this morning of all mornings? You want to think golf, old girl, right?"

"Right," Laurel echoed heartily.

"I'll be with you all the way," Webb said. "I know you're going to have a great round today. Elsie was telling me that rabbit of yours has some swing."

"Oh, he's a real swinger," Laurel deadpanned, to cover the sudden thumping of her heart.

Eyeing her curiously for a brief moment, Webb went on, "Not to hex you, but I've bet on the Doug Stewart foursome, and when I bet it's with my head, not my heart. I really do think you're going to finish in the money."

"With Jack Nicklaus and Tom Watson in the field today, I hope you got good odds!" Laurel said.

"Come on, Laurel. I know you a little. You're not going to tell me you're just going out there today for the fun of it."

Laurel playfully jabbed Webb's chest with her forefinger. "I would never try to tell you anything. Of course I'm going to play to win. I don't know how to play any other way. But at the same time, I hope you don't mind if I keep a little perspective."

They walked arm in arm into the grillroom, a spacious, walnut-paneled informal dining area decorated with prints depicting life on the golf links. Laurel knew the club gossips were taking note. To the public eye she and Webb were definitely an item. He had been a good friend and she always enjoyed their evenings together.

But this morning she found herself questioning the lack of intensity between them—a quality she'd previously taken comfort in. Though Webb had told her often enough that he found her beautiful, their sexual relationship had consisted exclusively of a few kisses that would have been acceptable in a "G"-rated movie. Doug Stewart, damn him, had achieved greater intimacy with her in a few flashing moments than Webb had in over a year.

Did she really want intimacy? Or was it the thing on earth that she dreaded the most?

Elsie Howard was signaling Laurel from a table for two out on the screened-in porch.

"See you on the course," she said to Webb.

"I'll be with you all the way," he repeated, adding, "Look, why don't I pick you up tonight and bring you back here for the cocktail party? Parking is going to be a nightmare, even with the extra attendants."

"That's sweet of you, Webb, but I've got a VIP sticker on my car because I'm playing today, so I'll get to use the side lot."

"In that case, why don't you pick me up?"

"All right," Laurel agreed, knowing she had no choice. Watching Webb head for a big table filled with the heaviest gamblers among the club membership, she bit back her resentment at the evening arrangement. She wouldn't have to go more than two blocks out of her way to pick up Webb, but she felt imposed upon nevertheless.

A fantasy suddenly broke loose from the storehouse within her mind. She saw Doug Stewart in the passenger seat of her gray Mercedes convertible, the two of them speeding away from Falling Water and the cocktail crowd, then spinning up Route 44 to Avon Mountain, parking at the notorious overlook to watch the darkening sky bring out the sparkling lights of downtown Hartford on the horizon. The skyline and the scented air of summer would enthrall them for a few minutes, then they'd turn one to another, unable to tolerate even the few inches between them. Doug would impatiently pull her out from behind the driver's seat, his hands caressing her everywhere on her body, his kisses forcing her head back against the maroon leather of the seats....

"I said, 'Good luck today, Laurel,'" a voice intruded waspishly, and Laurel came to.

"Thanks, Sara," she managed, bestowing a small smile on her forbidding, matriarchal sister-in-law. Sara was sitting at her usual table with her usual friends—a group of women Laurel and Elsie had privately dubbed the Iron Maidens, and not just because of their uniformly severe gray hairdos. Laurel knew that she was conservative in many areas, but Sara and her friends were positively reactionary. Sara had made it quite clear at the time of Laurel and Reed's wedding that she would never wholeheartedly welcome into the family a woman who had worked for a living, had no Colonial governors among her ancestors, and was marrying at age twenty-six after a suspiciously long season in her own apartment in downtown Hartford. Sara ran the powerful house committee of Falling Water and liked nothing better, Laurel thought, than to write letters to members rebuking them for letting young children run around the grillroom making *noise,* or—sin of sins—for setting foot in the poolside snack bar without proper tops over their swim togs.

"I'm surprised to see you here today," Laurel went on. "I'd assumed you'd be boycotting the Classic."

Sara grimaced at the inelegant word *boycotting.* Perfecting her already formidable posture, she said, "Quite the contrary. Once the board made its regrettable decision, it seemed imperative to *us* that *we* be on hand." She made a gesture encompassing the prim sisterhood at the table. "We're all markers today. In fact, when the lots were drawn yesterday, I got your foursome. You know how scrupulous I am about avoiding even the ap-

pearance of impropriety, so I checked with the committee—and they assured me that since the players themselves and not the markers are responsible for the
accuracy òf the scorecards, our relationship isn't rele-
vant."

"Besides," Laurel said, smiling sweetly, "no one
could possibly accuse you of favoritism on my behalf."

"The Campions have always been known for their
honesty," Sara returned stiffly.

Sighing inwardly, Laurel decided that a temporary
truce with her sister-in-law was probably more desirable
than the admittedly petty satisfaction of stinging her with
barbed comments. There would be enough distraction on
the course from Doug Stewart, not to mention the possibility of tension between Laurel and her stepson, Dean.
"I think this is going to be a great event for Falling
Water," she said genuinely, "and I'm glad you're going
to be part of it, Sara. We couldn't have asked for a more
glorious day to show off the course to the pros."

"Didn't you hear the latest forecast?" one of the Iron
Maidens put in, with gloomy satisfaction. "There's a
seventy percent chance of a thunderstorm this morning."

Laurel never blushed, but she did sometimes turn pale,
and she felt now as though the tan were being siphoned
out of her cheeks. She hurried away from the table before
she had to hear Sara remind her friend that thunderstorms
were a very touchy subject for Laurel. Every year golfers
were injured or killed by lightning on the course, and
two years earlier the grim statistics had included Reed
Campion, fatally struck down during a round in Ber-
muda, where he'd gone on a brief business trip.

Sliding onto a chair opposite Elsie, Laurel said miserably, "Did you hear? Seventy percent chance of a
thunderstorm this morning."

"I heard," Elsie said, "but come on, darling, since
when did you and I start believing weather forecasters?
I thought you rated them slightly below astrologers. That

sky is a very convincing shade of blue. I bet the storm misses us completely."

"I knew it was gustier than usual out there," Laurel lamented. She took a long draught of ice water from the goblet in front of her. "Elsie, if there's thunder—"

"If there's even a hint of thunder, you come straight in."

"That Doug Stewart isn't going to want to quit for anything. I can just hear his accusing me of being afraid I'll get my hair wet," she sighed. "Nothing's going to get him off the course except the official siren."

"That's *his* problem," Elsie said. "The rules are perfectly explicit. You want it, chapter and verse? Rule 37-6: 'The player shall not discontinue play on account of bad weather...unless he considers that there be danger from lighting.'"

Laurel couldn't help grinning. Elsie might be a Class C golfer, but she had a Class A grip on the complex laws governing the game. "You should be a referee today," she said.

"I'd much rather lead your cheering section and be your general manager. Right now my orders are: eat. How about a big glass of orange juice, followed by steak and eggs?"

"You just want some vicarious thrills," Laurel protested, looking pointedly at the cup of black coffee cooling in front of her friend. But she meekly obeyed orders and ate every scrap of the food served her.

After the good meal and Elsie's nonstop recitation of her twins' latest knock-knock jokes and other jewels of the eight-year-old mind, Laurel was feeling like her usual self, her winning self, as she started down to the first tee. Her equanimity was not ruffled by the sight of her sister-in-law wearing an unsmiling, officious face; nor by the sight of Dean, wearing—sure enough—jeans that didn't look fit for gardening in. Neither did the size of the crowd of friends and strangers, nor the presence of the sporting press. She wasn't even unnerved by the swaggering grin Doug Stewart gave her as he looked up from a conference with his caddy rigged out in the official purple jumpsuit, Doug's name on his back in yellow felt letters.

"So," Doug taunted, as she started to pass him on her way to Dean and her clubs, "you couldn't stay away. I bet you tried your damnedest, eh?"

"Not exactly," Laurel said coolly. She pointed to the chalkboard that posted the first initials and last names of the players teeing off at nine-fifty. "I'm L. Campion."

If the news threw Doug he concealed the fact behind laughter. "By God, you are, aren't you? *L* for Lady Blue?"

"*L* for Laurel," she corrected.

"Laurel!" he exclaimed mirthfully. "That's even better. Isn't the laurel the Connecticut state flower? Instant execution for anyone who lays a finger on it?"

"Connecticut is a progressive state," Laurel returned. "We won't execute you—just put you in a pillory for a few days."

Her joke had the opposite effect, turning his mood abruptly dark. "Never mind, Mrs. Campion," Doug muttered, "I'm fully aware that you're a protected species. I wouldn't touch you now if you asked me to."

The master of ceremonies announced Doug's name, a small ripple of applause broke out in the gallery, and Doug advanced to the tee, leaving Laurel to stare after him in a tumult of emotions.

chapter

3

LAUREL HIT A textbook drive off the first tee, sending her ball to the crook of the dogleg, only a few yards short of Doug's drive. She and Doug watched politely as Ed Collins and Murph Michaels hit off considerably less impressive shots. Ed and Murph were a pair of portly high handicappers, who usually limited themselves to nine-hole rounds and used an electric cart at that.

"I can't believe those guys are willing to play in front of a crowd," Dean remarked, shouldering Laurel's blue and white leather bag as he followed her down the fairway.

"'Those guys' may win us some holes," she reminded him. In a best-ball-of-four event, the lowest score shot by a member of a foursome on any given hole was the team score for that hole. The amateurs deducted strokes according to their handicaps, and Ed and Murph would be entitled to take off one or two strokes on every hole. "Anyway, I admire them for playing today. Unlike *some* people in the field, they don't think they're the greatest thing to swing a golf club since Ben Hogan retired." She raised her voice above its usual calm pitch, hoping the wind would carry her words down the fairway to Doug Stewart.

"I thought you were so gung ho on achievement," Dean said, with undisguised sarcasm.

Laurel looked at his fine featured face and straw-colored hair. Like his physical appearance, his character seemed to have more to do with the mother who had abandoned him than the father who had gone all out for him.

"I believe in giving your best effort to whatever you do," she said, "but that doesn't mean you only do what you can do well. I work hard at my golf game, and I get a lot of pleasure out of knowing I'm good at it. I also enjoy social dancing, for instance, though I wouldn't really be good at it if I took lessons for the next hundred years. But I *have* taken dance lessons and I'm afraid I've gotten as good as I can get. Both Mr. Collins and Mr. Michaels have taken golf lessons and practiced over and over."

"Your generation is hung up on lessons," Dean said querulously. "Look where your belief in authority figures has gotten the world. The pollution in our environment—"

"Dean," Laurel said, "I love our nightly political debates, but if you mention pollution or any other traumatic issues out here on the course today, I will strangle you." She gave his shoulder an affectionate jostle in an effort to brighten his glum expression. "I promise you that the globe will not be significantly worse off if you confine your attention to golf for the next few hours. What club do you think I should use?" she asked her stepson as they approached her ball.

"You know you want your five wood," Dean said, refusing to be humored. He removed the protective blue leather cap and handed her the club.

Laurel didn't like the way the shot seemed to pull, and she raised a tense left hand to shade her brow as she tracked the flight of the ball. A small whistle of irritation escaped her lips as the ball dropped to the apron, a few feet shy of the green. "A tad short," she said, frowning. She gave Dean her club, then ghosted a swing. *"That's* how I should have hit it. Lord, look at *his* shot." Doug had hit an effortless-looking nine iron that landed his ball on the green, pin high.

"What I don't understand," Dean said, "is why you say you enjoy a game that gets you so tense."

"Tension isn't the enemy in life," Laurel said. "Indifference is. Look . . . golf is a kind of metaphor. Every shot counts, just as it does out there." She made a sweeping gesture encompassing the world lying beyond the course. "I get tense because I care, and caring is what makes life worth living. How are you going to fight against pollution, for instance, unless you get tense about what's happening to the environment?"

Realizing that she'd violated her own edict against raising dire subjects, she burst into laughter. As Dean's laughter joined hers, she felt a rush of the affection he'd sorely tried lately with his negativism. If only, she thought irrationally, she could have come into his life in time to be a real mother figure. Instead she'd been installed in his house as the beautiful blond twenty-six-year-old wife of his forty-six-year-old father, just as Dean was entering the storm center called adolescence. "I guess you get to strangle me," she said, linking arms with him. "Will you stay my sentence until the match is over?"

Hearing applause from the second green, she realized that someone in the foursome ahead of hers must have sunk a tricky putt. The big names on the tour would be teeing off later in the morning, and the crowds would grow mammoth, but even now a swelling band of on-lookers was threading its way among the towering lindens and maples that dotted the rough and cast dramatic shad-ows across the lush fairways. Laurel waved at Elsie, highly visible in the red skirt she'd changed into, with lanky Webb Daniels who raised his hand in a victory sign. When Laurel was stroking the ball, the rest of the world ceased to exist, but as she walked the fairway, feeling exposed and vulnerable in the wide-open space, she was glad to know her cheering section was at hand.

"Get legs," she murmured in frustration, as her chip shot landed fifteen feet from the cup and then just sat there. Doug sank his second putt, getting the foursome off to a respectable start with a par 4, and Laurel knelt behind her ball to line up her own putt. Playing to a six handicap, she would be allowed to deduct a stroke from her gross score on this hole. If she sank her putt, the team would be off to a better than respectable start with a net birdie 3. "Do it for the Gipper," she heard Elsie say.

With a slight smile on her face, the image of Reed centermost in her mind, Laurel stroked the ball and ag-onized as it danced on the lip of the cup—then fell in. Buoyed by applause from the crowd and the excited congratulations from her teammates and their caddies, she hit a tee shot on the one-hundred-sixty-two-yard sec-ond hole that carried her ball to the heart of the green.

By the fifth hole, one of the longest on the course, when ungainly Murph Michaels chipped into the cup for a miraculous eagle 3, Laurel realized excitedly that both she and the foursome were playing sensational golf. Their tensions cast aside for the moment, she and Doug ex-changed triumphant glances. Her mind raced. Their foursome would win the event, and Doug would go on to win the Classic, and—

She felt rain.

She cocked an ear for thunder and studied the darkness of the clouds.

"What's up?" Doug asked.

"It's raining," Laurel said, forcing a smile.

Calmly holding out his big hand, he said, "So it is. Let's get to the sixth tee. Murph, you're going to dine out on that shot for years, eh?" He put a comradely arm around the portly businessman's shoulder, and for a moment Laurel cast her fears aside to revel in the display of Doug's good-heartedness. Traditionally, the men on the tour regarded pro-am events as all but insufferable, practice rounds at best, and were reportedly often brusque with their duffer teammates. Then the raindrops started getting fatter, and Laurel could no longer smile. She tugged at Doug's arm. "We have to go in." Dean was at the ball washer, and she motioned him over with a frantic wave. Surely he would be as unnerved as she by any hint of a thunderstorm on the course.

"I remembered to check that your umbrella was in the bag," Dean said proudly, apparently totally unconcerned. "You want your drizzler?" Taking her silence for assent, he got a lightweight pale-blue rain jacket from her bag and handed it to her.

"This is a great fashion show," Doug barked, "but the foursome behind us is about to putt, and if we don't tee off promptly, we could be hit with a two-stroke penalty."

Laurel stood paralyzed. Her frantic eyes searched the gallery, and she saw Elsie and Webb, who showed their concern. But concern didn't save people from lightning. Nothing did. She fumbled with her drizzler, forcing herself to breathe deeply, telling herself to take her example from Dean, who clearly couldn't have been less scared. But when had Dean known what to fear and what not to fear?

"Now," Doug said. He got hold of Laurel's elbow. Even in her agonized state, his touch was a source of exquisite heat, the faint spice of his aroma a key that threatened to unlock her storehouse of fantasies and let them all escape at once. "What's the matter with you, Lady Campion?" he hissed in her ear. "You afraid of getting your hair wet?"

She couldn't help laughing at the line she had perfectly predicted in conversation with Elsie, and somehow she got to the sixth tee and managed to hit a drive that although hardly the best in her golfing career at least wasn't the worst. Then the rain stopped, as abruptly as it had started, with the sky a flawless blue.

"You know what Mark Twain said about the New England weather," Laurel bubbled to Doug, giddy with relief. "If you don't like it, wait a minute!"

On the ninth hole, the rain came down again, in sheets. The gallery started to retreat. Neither Elsie nor Webb had rain gear with them, and Laurel emphatically motioned them back toward shelter. Sara Campion grimly tightened the hood on her drizzler, giving Laurel a look that seemed to say that the weather was fit punishment for those who had countenanced the invasion of Falling Water.

The rain lifted slightly, and Laurel breathed easier. Then a rumbling sound in the distance unnerved her so that she had to put her hand in her mouth to keep from screaming.

"Just a car backfiring out on Route 10," Murph Michaels told her, giving her a comforting pat. He had been a friend of Reed's and guessed what she was going through. "Don't worry. You'll hear that siren if there's even the slightest chance of lightning."

Laurel wished she shared his confidence, but she didn't. Of course no one on the committee running the tournament wanted to jeopardize the players, but golfers traditionally played through rain, and the committee wasn't likely to suspend the event unless there were unmistakable signs of danger.

Somehow she managed to get a birdie 3 on the tenth hole, a par 4 on the eleventh. Despite the extraordinary strain she was under—or perhaps because of it—she was playing one of the finest rounds of golf in her life.

She saw Doug staring at her as she tapped in her second putt on the eleventh, and she knew it wasn't just her stroke that was riveting him.

"So damn beautiful," he muttered, "with your hair getting wavy under that hood—" He broke off with one of his savage sneers. "Where is he?" he said.

"Who?"

"Your husband." He glared at the hardy few huddling under bright golf umbrellas in the rough. "That one in the purple jacket? No, you'd never allow a husband to wear purple."

Laurel simply stared at him, but a part of her exulted. He had said he wouldn't touch her again because he had seen her wedding ring. But she wasn't ready to reveal a technical accessibility that wasn't matched by an emotional one. "I wouldn't dream of telling a husband of mine what he was allowed to wear," she said coolly, then moved on toward the next tee before he could pin her with his hazel eyes and pull every last truth out of her.

The twelfth hole had given Falling Water its name, and, even through the slanting rain, Laurel thought it almost exotic in its beauty. The women's, men's, and championship tees for the hole were all on high ground, and a well-hit drive would sail across the tumbling brook that ran moatlike around the green.

In the mist Laurel had trouble tracking her shot, but she'd played the hole often enough to be certain her ball had landed on the near side of the water, down to the left. She asked Dean for her pitching wedge, the club she would need to loft a shot over the water, then she instructed him to carry her bag down the path and across the bridge that led to the right-hand side of the green. An abandoned snack bar between the twelfth green and the thirteenth tee would offer him some shelter against the rain. Not that any of them could get much wetter— and at least the rain was warm—but Dean had had too many colds that year, and Laurel instinctively made the maternal gesture.

As she stumbled down the rain-shrouded hill in search of her ball, Laurel was almost sorry she'd sent Dean off. For all the eerie mistiness of the day and the blurring of the familiar landscape, she might as well have been playing some strange heathery course off in Scotland. A part of her mind concentrated on finding her ball, while another part took note that her drizzler was thoroughly soaked. And still another portion floated free on one of her fantasies co-starring Doug Stewart: they'd just come off the famous St. Andrew's course in Scotland, and now they were back at their bed-and-breakfast inn. The proprietess was saying there was only enough hot water for one bath; Doug winked at Laurel and she knew he was thinking about a shared bath. Then the water was running, and he was undressing her, his hands urgent on the buttons of her shirt, wiggling teasingly under the lace of her bra.

A swelling roll of thunder wiped her mind clear of everything but terror. Blinded by the misting rain and her own fear, she couldn't see the abandoned snack bar, which was grounded against lightning and the only safe place around. The siren sounded to suspend play, its haunting wail mixing with her moans. She dropped her metal-shafted club and realizing she was only a few feet from water, started to run in the opposite direction, back up toward the twelfth tee.

"Laurel! Laurel!" Was that Doug's voice, rippling with concern for her, or was she in the grips of another fantasy? "Laurel, where are you?"

"Here!" she managed to call out, not knowing where here was but hoping her voice would act as a beacon. "I'm here!" Lightning split the sky overhead, and she stumbled, only to be caught up in strong arms.

"Laurel? Darling? It's all right, I've got you. I understand now—Murph told me everything. Why didn't you tell me what was wrong, you silly fool? Never mind, I've got you, and that's all that matters."

Laurel clung to him, letting him carry her. "Is Dean all right? Is everyone safe?"

"They're all in that snack bar, they're fine—" His voice trailed off as thunder rumbled, then roared. "We can't join the party, can we," he said conversationally, "because we'd have to cross water, so we have to think of something else." He rocked her and clutched her. "Can you collect yourself a bit and tell me the shortest way off the course? There must be farms bordering the club property—"

"Yes!" Laurel cried. "If we go way around to the left, the brook goes underground, there's the Epsteins' farm—"

"And Mark Twain once said, 'If you don't like the Epsteins' farm, wait a minute,'" Doug improvised inanely. "Can you run, or did you hurt your ankle back there?"

"I can run."

Hand in hand they streaked across the fairway, fleeing the thunder as if it were the booming cannons of war. Lightning sizzled above them, and just as Laurel was certain the next bolt would surely strike them, the bright red color of a barn loomed in the gray of the storm, and in seconds they were snug inside.

Laurel collapsed onto a pile of hay, disbelieving of the sweet warm scent rising around her, the dryness and the womblike safety of the loft they'd scrambled into. As her eyes adjusted to the dimness, she was able to gauge the depth of Doug's concern for her, and she reached out a hand to reassure him, to thank him.

He brought her hand to his lips, and, as the two of them simultaneously realized that the fingers he was about to kiss were still sheathed in the pale blue leather golf glove, they laughed. Their laughter turned into near hysteria, releasing their pent-up emotions over their brush with death. Then suddenly tears came streaming out of Laurel's eyes, and she turned away from Doug to sob heavily, releasing the deeper emotions she'd been unable to confront and express until this moment.

Seeming to understand that her tears were private and not connected with him, Doug reacted with a sensitivity she would not have dreamed was part of his emotional makeup. He refrained from speech and he refrained from touch, except for an occasional gentle stroking of her wet hair as her sobs diminished, then rose again.

Only when she had clearly unburdened herself and had turned faceup on her hillock of hay, offering him a tentative smile, did Doug say softly, "If you don't like the weather, wait a minute."

"Doug—" The rain on the roof of the barn filled the silence she created. Almost defiantly, she went on, "I was crying for Reed. My husband. I loved him, you know."

"I should hope so," Doug said. "I'd have to worry about a woman who lived with a man she didn't love." He added wearily, "I've known a few of those."

Tracing tender zigzags on his forearm, Laurel asked, "Have you loved?" Doug nodded. "Ever been married?" she asked, with an offhandedness she didn't remotely feel. Doug looked away, then back at her, his hazel eyes unreadable. "No," he said.

She wasn't quite sure whether she was surprised or not, reassured or not. "How old are you?" she asked, trying to cover the awkwardness of the moment.

"Thirty-seven. Pretty old for a rabbit, eh? And you? Twenty-six?"

"Thirty-two, and you know it."

A clap of thunder shook the barn, and lightning flashed so close by that an unearthly brilliance seeped between the boards of the barn walls. Involuntarily starting toward Doug, Laurel found him gathering her up in an embrace that began as shelter and quickly turned into something very different.

"We could go on asking each other questions, Lady Blue," he whispered huskily, "like where were you born, and what was the name of your kindergarten teacher, and—" His words were lost in a kiss that turned every inch of Laurel's body into fevered, pulsing, hungry flesh. She moaned his name over and over as he covered her body with his own, letting her feel his strength and his desire for her, turning the hay beneath her into the most exquisite of beds.

"Am I crushing you?" he asked, running fingers through her wet hair, splaying it on the hay, raining kisses on her eyelids, her cheeks, her nose, her chin, the silken tautness of her throat.

"No. Yes. Crush me," she answered, clasping her hands around his neck, arching up at him, exuberantly telegraphing her pleasure in his muscular body, his demanding mouth.

"We'll catch pneumonia in these wet clothes," Doug murmured, eyeing Laurel as though expecting her to turn from him, from her own desire. Instead, she heaved toward him, offering the buttons of her white knit shirt to his eager fingers, a smile of satisfaction lighting her face as his hazel eyes took in the creamy swell of her skin beneath the intricate lace of her bra.

"Such a surprising woman," Doug shook his head in wonder as his fingers teasingly worked their way under her bra, just as they had done in Laurel's fantasy. "All that gorgeous lace under that awful shirt. What do I dare hope she's wearing under the awful skirt?"

Laurel's giggles turned to groans of pleasure as his

fingers found her nipples, and his lips once again crushed down on her lips. His fingers were on the button at the waist of her skirt when a loud banging noise intruded—not thunder this time, but the sudden opening of the barn door.

"Shep?" a woman's voice called. "Shep? Are you in here, boy? Shep?"

Realizing that she had a few moments' grace while the woman's eyes adjusted to the dimness of the barn, Laurel hastily buttoned up her shirt.

"Shep?" The woman whistled. "Here, boy. Here, boy." Then, straining into the gloom, she said, "Hello? Is someone up in the loft?"

Drawing breath, Laurel called down, "Mrs. Epstein? Hi, it's Laurel Campion from Falling Water. We got caught out on the twelfth hole when the thunder started and ran here for shelter. I hope you don't mind. This is Doug Stewart, one of the pros in the Classic," she added, bestowing her best social smile on the round-faced Mrs. Epstein as the latter's eyes focused.

"Goodness, Mrs. Campion, are you all right? You should have come to the house."

"We took the first shelter we could find," Laurel said, not adding that she and Doug hadn't been looking for company. "I hope you'll forgive us for trespassing.

"Don't be silly. Why you golfers play in the rain is beyond me. Of course, why you play under the best of conditions is beyond me too, so what do I know? Come on down, and I'll get you some dry clothes up at the house. You've got just about the figure of my eighteen-year-old daughter, and I expect there's something of my husband's that Mr.—"

"—Stewart," he growled. "Doug Stewart."

"—that Mr. Stewart will fit into."

As they crossed from barn to house, a soaking wet miserable-looking sheep dog came dashing out from under some bushes, trying vainly to shake the water from his matted hair.

"Shep! There you are, boy!" Mrs. Epstein knelt in the mud to comfort the dog, then led her bedraggled crew into the back hall of her rambling white farmhouse. "I'll be back in a minute with towels and clothes, then we'll see about some hot tea," she said, leaving Laurel and Doug to take off their grass-caked shoes.

As the gray-haired woman bustled out of sight, Laurel turned to Doug with a mischievous grin. To her astonishment, his thick eyebrows were raised to their most scornful height, his mouth was curled in his favorite one-sided sneer.

"Rescued just in the nick of time, eh, Lady Blue?"

chapter

4

REED HAD INSTALLED a whirlpool tub in the spacious blue-tiled master bath of the house on Main Street, and a half-hour soak in the invigorating waters was usually tonic enough for Laurel even after the most grueling day of competitive golf. But today as she positioned her aching shoulder muscles to take the full thrust of the powerful water jets, she realized that the strain of the extraordinary day she'd just lived through wasn't about to wash away. She lay her blond head on a plastic pillow that bobbled on the surface of the water, closed her eyes, inhaled the deep-sea scent of the mineral salts she used, and tried to make her mind a blank. No luck. Image after image from the tumultuous day at Falling Water leaped to mind, clamoring for her attention.

Stronger even than the indelible image of jagged white

lightning skewing the sky was the image of Doug
Stewart's stormy face when she'd turned to him in the
back hallway of Mrs. Epstein's farmhouse. Mrs. Epstein
had returned with towels and dry clothing before Laurel
could begin to query Doug's retreat from tenderness.
They were never alone with each other, able to talk, from
that moment on. No sooner had they changed—in separate rooms—and had a few restorative sips of tea with
Mrs. Epstein than the freak storm had lifted and they'd
heard the siren blow to announce the resumption of play
in the Classic. Doug had charged back out to the course,
his long-legged stride keeping him yards ahead of Laurel
until they rejoined the other members of their foursome
and the supporting crew of caddies and marker. Any
words they had exchanged for the rest of the round were
strictly limited to the game at hand. On the long
seventeenth hole—one of the holes on which Laurel,
with her six handicap, got a stroke—she had sunk her
second putt for a net birdie 4, doing more for the team
than Doug with his par 5; his sole comment had been an
unmistakably sardonic "Congratulations."

Turning the water as hot as her skin could bear it, she
mentally relived their stolen moments of passion in the
barn, wondering frantically whether she had done something to turn him off. But what? She'd unstintingly offered herself up for their shared pleasure. Sighing, she
decided she'd been dead right in her first assessment of
him as a wildly dangerous being who could be relied
upon to snarl without provocation if his unruly spirit so
moved him. Just as well, then, that Mrs. Epstein had
interrupted their hot embrace before he had taken total
possession of her. But, oh Lord, how she had wanted
that ultimate joining. As her hands soaped her round
breasts, then worked their way down her slim body, she
slipped into another of her fantasies: it was Doug's hands
that teased her intimately with soap, making her completely aware of her every swell and curve.

Aghast, she flung the soap away, virtually hurdled herself out of the tub, and toweled herself dry with a punitive roughness. How could she indulge in lascivious fantasies about Doug Stewart while lying in the tub that Reed had bought for her—had bought for *them?* True, he'd never thought of it as an erotic toy, any more than he would have been party to a literal roll in the hay in Mrs. Epstein's barn. Their lovemaking, while warm and satisfying, had always had a rather ceremonial air to it, almost a kind of formality. Thinking back, Laurel realized that she and Reed had never made love anywhere other than in their four-poster bed, with its monogrammed ice-blue sheets and royal-blue silk coverlet, a pewter pitcher of water on his bedside table, a pale blue enameled box of tissues on hers.

Laurel looked in the full-length mirror on the bathroom door and decided that she was looking at a traitor. How she despised the women at the club whose locker-room chat was full of snide remarks about their husbands—about how this one was tight with money, and that one didn't take any interest in the children, and that one fell asleep the minute he was done with lovemaking, sometimes the minute before he was done. To join the ranks of those women even in the privacy of her mind seemed an unbearable insult to Reed, to herself. And yet—wasn't it a kind of insult to the marriage to have to pretend it had been a union of superbeings? "Be honest!" the damp blonde in the steamy mirror exhorted her. "It was a marriage of two human beings, and nothing human is perfect. It was a wonderful marriage—but it wasn't the first wonderful marriage, or the last. There might even be another, very different, wonderful marriage for you."

Laurel stuck her tongue out at the mirror and turned away. Lord, how confusing life could be, even when you were famous for your orderly, rational mind! Anyway, what difference did it make whether she accepted her steamy longing for Doug or rejected it? He quite clearly had lost whatever momentary interest he had had in her.

Nonetheless she decided not to wear the long-sleeved, white-collared blue chiffon cocktail dress that Reed had admiringly called "secretly sexy." Something fire-engine red and slit down to her navel was more likely to appeal to Doug, and—damn him—she did want to appeal to him. Not owning anything red and breathtakingly bare, Laurel dug out a blue, green, and violet print chiffon with spaghetti straps and a softly swirling skirt. It left a little guesswork in the bosom department, but with strappy French lavender kid sandals on her feet, her legs would be very much on display. She'd impulsively bought the dress in Boca Raton that winter, worn it once to dinner, and then, returning north, buried it in the farthest reaches of her closet. It was hardly the sort of thing she wanted to wear on her chaste outings with Webb Daniels, or for the Farmingdale summer party circuit.

She laid the chiffon confection on her bed and went to her dressing table. She picked up her hair blower, then put it down. The hair she had washed and toweled, then left to air dry as she vainly pursued relaxation in the tub, was a soft mass around her face. Doug—damn him, double damn him—had found her beautiful when the rainstorm on the course undid her sleek pageboy and revealed the secret of her natural waves. She ran a brush through her hair, pushed it about with her fingers, and left it to finish drying while she applied moisturizer and a translucent foundation onto her face. Studying the finished result after she stroked delicate touches of pink to her cheeks and lips and a suggestion of violet to her eyelids, she decided that she'd do. On second glance, remembering the sneering curl to Doug's lips, she decided to tame her hair with a tortoiseshell comb. He could have her if he whistled—damn him—but she didn't have to announce the fact in neon. Especially not if her efforts to entice him went unrewarded.

She knocked on Dean's door. "Dean? Ready to go?"

He opened the door, wearing a pair of cutt-offs and a T-shirt. "I'm not going, Laurel. Hey, you look terrific. What did you do to your hair?"

"It's what I didn't do." She entered his room, a typical teen haven—rock posters on the walls, clothes strewn everywhere, stereo and television both on, though at least at a low decibel level. "Why aren't you coming to the party? Don't you want to be part of the glory? You certainly deserve to be."

Their foursome had tied for third with a nine-under-par 63—a very pleasant fact that had been relegated to the back of Laurel's mind in the past hour. Doug Stewart would receive a cash prize at the cocktail party, and the amateurs would get lavish gifts from the pro shop.

Sinking moodily onto his unmade bed, Dean said, "I'm just too pooped. I thought a shower would pick me up, but it didn't. It's hard work, lugging around clubs. I'm glad I don't have to be a caddy for a living."

"You did work hard out there," Laurel said, sitting next to him. "You were just super, kiddo—but you're not going to tell me that if an old lady like me could pull herself together for the party, you can't. I bet Ginny Demerest will be pretty crushed if you don't show up." When Dean didn't say anything, she added, "Is it the business with the cars? I didn't mean to pressure you about coming over with Webb and me, but it seemed so much more sensible, considering the parking situation." Tousling Dean's straw-colored hair, she added with a smile, "And of course it's much kinder to the environment if we go in one car. But come in your own car if it makes you happier."

Dean looked away. "It's not the car. I'm wiped out, honest."

"What will you do about dinner?"

"Make a salad or something—I've been thinking

about becoming a vegetarian."

Biting back a smile, Laurel stood up and dropped a kiss on his head. "You're the boss, kiddo. I bought some tomatoes from Epsteins'—they're on the window sill in the kitchen. They look great. Oh, and I got some fresh pasta from that new place in West Hartford—Nanshe's. It's in the freezer. Boil up a big pot of water, and then it only needs three minutes. Don't worry, it's all natural," she added, making a little face.

"You're wonderful," Dean flung himself down against his pillow.

"I'm not, either. I'm your wicked stepmother." Sitting down again on the unmade bed, she said, "Are you sure you don't want to tell me what's on your mind? Hey," she added lightly, "now here's a turnabout. You clamming up, and me urging you to spill your guts. This offer may not be repeated. Void where prohibited by law."

His voice muffled by the pillow, Dean said, "Are you going to move to Toronto?"

"Am I *what?*"

"Are you going to move to Toronto?" Dean repeated.

"Why on earth would I do that?" she asked, though her heart could think of one very good reason for such a move.

"Come on, Laurel," Dean said, turning faceup. He tried for a grin and a joke. "You know how we teenagers are—all antennae." He waggled his fingers. "I think you and Doug Stewart caused that lightning with one of your smoldering glances."

"Dean, Dean." Laurel let out a great sigh, not sure whether to laugh or cry, whether to congratulate her stepson on his perceptiveness or call him on his freshness.

"I think he's terrific," Dean said. "Not that you asked for my blessing, but I think he'd make a good successor to Dad. I like Mr. Daniels, but he's not exactly, well, you know—" His eyes growing misty, he said, "Did you notice how Mr. Stewart's swing looks like Dad's? I didn't say anything to you out on the course because I didn't want to throw you off your game—but wow. That full shoulder turn, the high finish—"

"I know," Laurel said, staring off into the middle distance. She twisted the long rope of pearls she was wearing around her neck. "Now listen to me, Dean," she said, looking down at him. "First of all, you're going way too fast. I mean it. I'm a different generation. *We* don't go to Toronto on the basis of smoldering glances. Second—and get this through your head—if and when the time comes when I want to marry again, you damn well better believe I'll ask for your blessing. Which leads us to the third point. You're my family. We've had our rough moments lately, but that's part of being family instead of acquaintances, taking each other seriously. Remember what I was telling you today about tension? Well, there's tension between us because we count with each other. In other words, kiddo, you're not getting rid of me so easily. Any man who has the good fortune to get me has the good fortune to get you—until if and when you decide you want to leave the nest. Want to come to the party now? I'll give you five minutes to dress."

"I still think I'll pass on it," Dean said, sitting up, "but I sure feel a lot better. I might even postpone being a vegetarian. Are there any steaks in the freezer?"

"I'll take one out for you on the way down." Laurel stood up, smoothing her skirt. "This room is a mess. Why don't you do something with it while you're waiting for the steak to defrost?" She added merrily, over her shoulder, as she started out, "See what you're stuck with? Are you sure that business about Toronto wasn't wishful thinking on your part?"

"Positive," Dean called after her.

Laurel was still glowing when she pulled her Mercedes up in front of the blue eighteenth-century salt-box that Webb Daniels had inherited from his parents.

Laurel had heard the club gossips speculate about why he had never asked a woman to share the house—one theory holding that he was in love with a New York lawyer who refused to give up her practice and her penthouse in exchange for country-club life; another less savory theory holding that he gambled well beyond the country-club level and had no other real love. In keeping with their unstated covenant, Webb had never confided in Laurel, and she had never asked questions; but this evening, as she watched him lock his front door and start toward her car she felt a desire to break the agreement. Lord, how good it had felt to talk head on with Dean instead of running from emotion as she so often had. Maybe lightning *had* struck her on the course, she was beginning to think, so radically had she changed in a few hours.

"Well, counselor," she began lightly, as they drove toward Falling Water, "I took your advice out there today."

"You mean opening up your stance on your long irons?"

"I mean opening up my heart. While I was cowering from the storm, I finally had that big cry over Reed that you recommended."

Reaching out to touch her hand on the steering wheel, Webb said, with a huskiness that surprised her, "That's wonderful news, old girl. And is that daring dress of yours the result?"

"Not exactly—well, maybe," she hedged, not quite ready to be completely truthful. Dean, with his teenage "antennae," had guessed at her feelings for Doug Stewart, but that didn't mean the adult population of Falling Water had. No point in broadcasting her attraction to him unless there was some solid news to go with it.

"Now it's your turn in the confessional, Webb," she said, forestalling any questions he might put forth. "We've been friends for a while, right? So tell me.

What's the secret behind your bachelorhood? I gather the bars in downtown Hartford have gotten pretty swinging lately, but this isn't the best part of the world to be on your own in—as I know too well," she added.

"Oh, the usual story," Webb said, brushing back the shock of hair that was no less boyish for being gray.

"Which usual story?" Laurel pressed, as she shifted down to take the old iron bridge across the Farmingdale River. Below them, a couple of twilight anglers were casting for trout.

"First I was all caught up in law and politics—I don't know if you remember, but I made a run a while back for the state legislature. Then when I got rid of that bug, damned if I didn't fall in love with the new young wife of one my closest friends."

"Someone I know?" Laurel asked, her eyes widening. Then, ashamed, she immediately said, "Sorry, Webb. That was beastly. I withdraw the question."

"I'll answer it anyway," he said lightly. "You know her very well."

"I do? And did she fall in love with you? Oh, poor Webb, how ghastly for everyone."

"Only ghastly for me. I never let on for a minute. Even when the woman's husband died, I went on playing the old family friend because the woman was still too clearly in love with her husband to think seriously about another man. Then tonight, I saw a ray of hope."

"Tonight?" Laurel stammered, her chest constricting.

"Tonight—when she came to pick me up in the wildest dress I've seen in Greater Hartford, and gave me cause to believe that she'd finally truly buried her husband."

Speechless for a long moment, Laurel finally groaned, "Dear Webb."

"Don't worry, old girl. I'm not about to leap on you and press you to name the date. Nor will I remind you that your eyes are exactly the blue of my house and I've dreamed of moving you and Dean into that house. I've waited this long, I can wait a little longer. You obviously had some kind of revelation out there on the course, but I know how genuinely reserved you are, and I'm not deluded enough to think you're more than begun to open up to new possibilities. Believe me, your conservative nature is one of the things I cherish in you. Such a rarity in these times," he murmured, bending over to plant a small, respectful kiss on her bare shoulder.

Laurel's mind went into overdrive as she started up the long drive leading to the porte cochere outside the clubhouse. There an attendant would take over behind the wheel and whisk her car around to the small side lot reserved for those with the purple and yellow VIP tournament stickers. How could she disillusion Webb without bruising him? She thought back over the six years she had known him, wondering how a man could love a woman all that time and leave no clues. Had she unthinkingly stimulated him with the meaningless flirting indulged in by everyone at Falling Water? She hoped not. Webb was a good friend and she wouldn't want to cause him pain.

A score of friends hailed them as they entered the clubhouse and headed toward the main dining room. It seemed to Laurel that virtually the entire club membership had turned out for the gala event and the chance to raise glasses with some of the big stars in the golf world. People she scarcely knew congratulated her on the success of her foursome that day.

She dutifully kissed Evan Campion as Webb exchanged the ritual peck with Sara.

"Aren't you afraid you'll catch cold in that dress, dear?" Evan asked, trying unsuccessfully for airy joviality. But at least he tried, Laurel thought—unlike Sara, who stood there in a cap-sleeved, formless white pique dress, beaming tight-lipped disapproval Laurel's way. Evan was tall, thin, and silvery haired, and there the resemblance to his late younger brother ended. His face had an unwholesome flush from the screwdrivers he drank nonstop—once causing Elsie Howard to say to Laurel that if the vodka didn't do him in, he'd probably expire from an overdose of vitamin C in all that orange juice. He wasn't made any more impressive by the madras sport coat and red linen slacks he wore—another classic East Coast country-club summer costume donned in one variation or another by half the men present, including Webb. Laurel found herself wondering what Doug would wear that night, and her blue eyes swept the dining room for him.

"Looks damn nice here tonight, doesn't it?" Webb said proudly.

"Beautiful!" Laurel exclaimed automatically. Most of the dining tables had been removed, leaving a wide open space in the middle of the room for milling and mingling; the few tables to each side of the room were skirted with yellow cloths and sported tall arrangements of fragrant deep purple lilacs. A buffet table at the far end of the room was laden with whole cold poached salmon, iced shrimp, a rare filet of beef that a waiter was carving paper thin and offering up on crustless rounds of bread, and a bright array of vegetables steamed just long enough to bring out their color. Near the bar, a small round dance floor had been installed, and a pianist and bass player in white dinner jackets were playing the eternal favorites—"Where or When," "I Don't Know Why," "Can This Be Love?"

"When I look into your eyes," Webb said tenderly, whirling her onto the dance floor before she could protest, "I feel as though all these songs were written just for us."

"Please don't," Laurel murmured, suppressing a wave of misery, knowing guiltily that Webb would mistake her words for that reticence he cherished in her. Where, oh where, was Doug? What if he'd fallen asleep in his hotel room in downtown Hartford? What if he'd decided he had no use for a country-club cocktail party? What if he showed up and offered Laurel nothing more than a sneer?

She closed her eyes, letting Webb guide her, giving herself up to a fantasy: the arms around her were Doug's powerful arms, and it was Doug's breath in her hair, Doug's hardness against her body, Doug's deep, lilting voice saying—

"May I?"

Her eyes flew open as Doug tapped Webb on the shoulder to cut in. Introducing the two men, Laurel drank in Doug's looks—raffish yet elegant in a camel-color sport coat too soft to be anything but cashmere. With a start, she realized that he'd had his hair cut in the brief time that they'd been apart; he still wore it longer than most of the members of Falling Water, but it was no longer an adolescent boast of indifference to grooming. Almost shy, not wanting him to think she thought he'd had his hair cut to please her, she told him how handsome he looked.

"And you look gorgeous," he growled, "or you would—if you didn't hedge the bet. You're a great one for bet hedging, eh, Lady Blue?" He boldly plucked the tortoiseshell comb out of her hair so that its soft waves fell free, then put the comb in his pocket. "So this is how you get yourself up for one Webb Daniels," he said. Holding her at arms' length, he commented, "Lucky fellow. After getting a taste of your favors, I envy him— almost."

Was everyone going to misconstrue her that evening? "Listen to me, you silly man," she cried softly, "do you really think it was Webb Daniels I had in mind when I put on this dress?"

"If not the dapper Mr. Daniels, then who?" Breaking off their dance, he kept an arm around her waist as he stood on the edge of the dance floor and took stock of the crowd. "Who in the midst of all this conspicuous consumption has your heart, Lady Blue? And that exquisite body of yours?" The sounds of the music and the chattering crowd rose and fell around them. "That portly gentleman with the portly cigar? Or the red-faced gentleman who's staring at us in consternation?"

"The man with the cigar happens to be a judge who is famous throughout the area for his fairness," Laurel said coldly. "And the red-faced man has his problems, but he really is a gentleman. I should know—he's my brother-in-law. Do you know what you are, Doug Stewart? You're an inverse snob. You can't believe anyone who has money might also happen to have brains and character and a good heart."

"So that's what I am," Doug answered, with heavy sarcasm, tightening his hold on her as the pianist and bass player struck up a medly of current hit songs. "It's always so useful to have insights into your psyche from someone who's known you a few hours." His body urged her into a faster rhythm. "Know something, Lady Blue? For someone who's a first-rate athlete and great in the hay, you're a lousy dancer."

Astonishing them both, Laurel burst into laughter. "Lord, Doug, if I have to be lousy in one of those three areas, didn't I pick the right one?"

"Laurel, Laurel," Doug groaned, crushing her to him as if the music were playing for them alone and the rest of the world had vanished, "I'm falling in love with you, and I can't bear it."

"Is love such an ordeal?" Laurel asked, over the thumping of her heart.

"With you—" he began, breaking off as Elsie Howard, wearing her "skinny-little-nothing" dress from London, whirled by in the arms of her tall, dark-haired husband, Pete.

Performing introductions, Laurel noticed the scowl on Doug's face.

"You get a kick out of it, don't you?" he said accusingly, as the Howards moved across the dance floor.

"Out of what?" she asked.

"Introducing me to your proper friends. Like Lady Chatterley, flaunting her gamekeeper, eh? I've never seen such a woman for introductions. This afternoon, in that barn, you hardly stopped to button up your shirt before you were introducing me to your precious Mrs. Epstein. I won't be used that way, damn you. Once was enough. Find yourself some other jock to toy with before you settle down with the proper lawyer."

Letting go of her, he would have left her stranded on the dance floor if she hadn't reached out and caught his arm. "And if I didn't introduce you to people?" she demanded. "What would you think then? You are the most infuriating combination of superiority and inferiority I've ever encountered."

"Like I said, Lady Blue, you can keep your insights. Thanks for your help on the course today."

Numbly Laurel watched him stride over to a gaggle of pretty college girls, say something that set them all to laughing, then escort the prettiest of the lot, Lucy Webster, onto the dance floor. Laurel danced with Webb again, and with Pete Howard, then got a glass of white wine from the bar and wandered out to the screened porch on the far side of the buffet table.

Like a small girl, she pressed her nose to the screen and stared out at the tranquil emptiness of the eighteenth green. Behind her the sounds of merriment escalated to fever pitch, but it did not summon her back; she was content to listen to the chirping crickets out on the course. The sun was beginning to sink beyond the practice tee, where only that morning she'd encountered a man who was capable of carrying her to soaring heights and sending her plummeting to nightmarish depths, sometimes within the same breath. Lord, oh Lord. Well, in three days the Classic would be done with, and he'd be off to the next event on the tour—to play his diabolical games with some other blond low handicapper. She grimly wondered if he'd left a trail of confused country-club widows all over the country. What real or imagined slights had he received in his life to mistake the social amenities for some unforgivable kind of insult?

Running a fingernail over the screen, she thought ahead to the future, trying to picture herself as chatelaine of Webb Daniels's blue saltbox. He would be good to her and devoted to Dean, but—no. She simply didn't want to be the woman Webb wanted her to be. With a little laugh she decided that maybe the fates had sent Doug Stewart her way to prevent an alliance she might otherwise have thought was everything she could now hope for from life.

The music ceased behind her, and she heard someone tapping on a microphone and saying, "Testing, one, two, three. Testing, one, two three." Realizing that the prizes for the pro-am tournament were about to be handed out, she started back into the main room, as determined to keep away from Doug as she'd earlier been eager to set eyes on him. She donned her mask of coolness and serenity, squared her shoulders, and joined Elsie and Pete at their lilac-bedecked table.

If her friends saw beneath her mask to her roiling emotions, they refrained from comment, for which reticence she was more than a little grateful. She suffered silently through speeches by the chairman of the board of Inner City Youth and the president of Falling Water; she cut herself off from the emotional impact in the love song belted out by Dahlia Stephens, a talented blues singer who had once been an ICY camper and now gave ten percent of her considerable annual earnings to that charitable organization. She applauded vigorously as two of the great touring pros and their local amateur colleagues stepped to the improvised podium to receive their prizes as first and second low scorers in the best-ball event, and made brief speeches of thanks.

Then she was at the receiving end of the applause as she, Murph Michaels, Ed Collins, and Doug Stewart were called to the front of the room as third-place winners. She kissed club pro Buzz Newfield on the cheek as he handed her a handsome pair of blue and white Footjoy golf shoes and a dozen Max-Fli balls, her favorite. Putting her booty down, she impulsively hugged Murph and Ed, who looked as though they'd been transported to heaven. She offered her best social smile and a firm New England hand to Doug, when he turned from the microphone after thanking the other members of his foursome and his caddy.

His hazel eyes swept over her composed face. Without any warning, he put his hands on Laurel's shoulders and brushed her lips in the gentlest of kisses, drawing cheers from the high-spirited crowd. Wounded by his tenderness as she would not have been by a bruising kiss, Laurel summoned her powers of self-control to maintain her calm facade. She kept her head high and her mouth fixed in a light smile as she stepped down from the podium, acting for all the world as though nothing extraordinary had happened. As she rejoined an openly grinning Elsie Howard, Laurel realized that in the strain of keeping Doug Stewart and the watching world from knowing how his kiss had inflamed and unsettled her, she had left behind her new golf shoes and golf balls. On the verge of asking Pete Howard to save her the embarrassing trip back to the podium, she saw Doug negotiating through the crowd waving her prizes.

"Thank you," she said simply. Looking around, she hesitated. She didn't want to plunk shoes and balls down on a table laden with drinks and half-eaten broccoli flowerets, and she didn't want to shove her winnings under the table only to forget them. She had money enough to buy out the supply of shoes and balls in the pro shop many times over, but her one superstition was that there were lucky powers in golf paraphernalia won, not bought. "I think I'll put these in my car," she told Elsie and Pete. "I could use a bit of air, anyway."

"It sure is stuffy in here," Doug agreed, his cocky grin making it apparent that he fully meant the words to reflect his opinion of the crowd as well as the smoky air. "I think I'll keep you company."

Determined not to give him the satisfaction of knowing how he irritated her, Laurel nodded and started toward the lobby, a neutral smile on her face. Equally determined not to let him know how she longed to be alone with him in the sultry Connecticut evening, she slowed their progress by pausing to introduce Doug to one of her favorite local pros, Frank Sarro from Tumblebrook Country Club in nearby Simsbury, and to Ginny Demerest, a snubnose, red-headed sixteen-year-old who asked wistfully after Dean.

"There must be one or two people back there you didn't introduce me to," Doug said gratingly, as they hit open air.

"I hope you don't feel slighted," Laurel said, affecting a wide-eyed innocence. "We'll catch up with them later." She called out to the parking lot attendant under the porte cochere that she was going to put something in her car, and then started down a gravel path to the side lot.

"I thought you'd be driving a Mercedes," Doug said with a smirk, as they got to her sleek gray convertible. "And there are sirloins in the freezer, eh? And every single one of those pearls around your neck was once on intimate terms with an oyster. Did Mummy and Daddums start you on the pearls when you were born?"

"Hah," Laurel said inelegantly, flashing back to her jewelless youth, as she put her trophies in the car. She slammed the door for punctuation. "I repeat, Doug Stewart, you are the worst snob I have ever known. You have the simplistic values of a teenager. The way you see things, the world is divided up into the evil rich and the noble poor, right? A lot you know."

To her amazement, he didn't parry her thrust; he groaned as though mortally wounded. "I only know one thing," he said. "I want you, and I'm going to have you, and it's going to be on my turf and my terms, do you understand me?" His arms went around her as his lips took complete possession of her lips, burning her mouth with the heat of his desire, cutting off any response she might have made, forcing open the gates to her body and her soul.

chapter

5

THE UNMISTAKABLE SOUND of teenage snickering brought the tempestuous embrace to a quick halt.

"Just my luck, they're friends of Dean's," Laurel said, moving away from Doug and peering about the parking lot. In the deepening twilight she had trouble picking out faces, but she was pretty sure she spotted Ginny Demerest's bright red hair. Not caring that her own face reflected her discomfort, she said, "I think one of them is Dean's girl."

"I suspect that Dean and his girl know all about kissing," Doug said, folding his powerful arms across his chest. His deep voice grated, "Or is it just that you only like to be seen kissing lawyers?"

Her body still feeling the imprint of his, her lips still tasting his mouth, Laurel decided to move toward peace,

not war. "You have something against lawyers?" she
asked lightly.

"It so happens I do," Doug growled enigmatically—
but at least his anger was directed at a person or persons
unknown, not at her. As a car sped out of the parking
lot, he said, more amiably, "Well, there go our chap-
erones."

"It *must* have been Ginny Demerest," Laurel mused.
"Her father played in the event today but didn't come
to the party, and I think she had his car with the VIP
sticker." Then, as Doug's words penetrated, a sudden,
inexplicable shyness hit her, and she retreated to formality. "Would you like a ride to your hotel?" she asked
Doug, "Or do you have a rented car?"

"Murph Michaels gave me a ride out. I told him I'd
find my way back. Actually, Lucy Webster offered me
a lift back."

"I see," Laurel said, turning away, opening her car
door. "I didn't realize she was old enough to drive. Good
night."

"Now, now, Lady Blue," Doug said, his strong hand
arresting her movement. "I said she'd offered. I didn't
say I'd accepted." Chuckling, he added, "You become
sublimely silly when you're upset. You know perfectly
well she's old enough to drive. A college woman. But
I'd love to ride with you, thank you."

As they got into the car Laurel said guiltily, "I feel
as though I'm running out on the parking attendant."

"Oh, he'll survive without your dollar, Lady Campion. Lord, I don't suppose you have any idea what it's
like to work for tips, eh? If there's a more degrading
connection possible between human beings, I don't know
what it is. When you're working for tips, you can't so
much as smile without mentally translating into cash.
And of course the person you're working for knows that
and suspects every smile."

Thinking back to her college years, when she had

worked as a waitress to pay for her education, Laurel remembered all too well the number of times she had bestowed an unfelt smile or wore a saucy rose pinned to her frilly uniform blouse, in hopes of getting bigger tips. A retort on her lips, she turned to Doug. Suddenly an idea struck, and she merely nodded. Instead of telling him about her waitressing days, she'd show him! "Next stop, Farmingdale River Inn," she said gaily, as she started down the steep Falling Water driveway.

"Farmingdale River Inn?"

"It's a restaurant, actually, despite the name—known for such New England favorites as mashed turnips and Indian pudding. But that's not why I'm taking you there. They have a very lively cocktail lounge."

"You're full of surprises, Lady Blue. I hope I won't let you down. I don't drink when I'm playing the next day."

"Have a ginger ale," Laurel said tartly. "One of the advantages of being out with women older than Lucy Webster is that they don't need their escorts to drink macho drinks. You can have a Shirley Temple, for all I care."

"What on earth is a Shirley Temple?"

"Ginger ale with a single drop of bitters, served in an old fashion glass with a maraschino cherry and a slice of orange," Laurel reeled off. "Usually served to the under-ten set, but be my guest."

"Let's get one thing straight," Doug said. "You'll be *my* guest, so don't start flashing your gilt-edged credit cards."

Smiling, Laurel said, "Don't worry, boss."

"'Boss,' eh? You think I'm too rough on you?"

"Now why do you say that?" Laurel asked, feigning amazement. "I've never had an easier time with anyone." Flicking on her turn indicator, she stopped for a light at the crossroad of Route 10 and Farmingdale River Road. "Dean thinks I'm politically stuffy," she commented, "but it does bring out the anarchist in me to stop for a light when there isn't another car around for miles. Why can't they have a blinking yellow?"

"I'll tell you why." Doug leaned over and rained hot little kisses on her lips, cheeks, chin, and pulsing throat.

Straining toward him, Laurel let her left foot come up off the clutch, and the idling car jerked and stalled. As the light turned green and she started again, she remembered her fantasy of parking with Doug, like two passionate, reckless teenagers, on the top of Avon Mountain. If the top weren't down, she thought, she'd be consumed by fire—after a minute's worth of kisses! Lord only knew what kind of inferno would rage if the two of them ever had an uninterrupted half hour. Tempted to head toward Route 44 and Avon Mountain, she decided instead to stick to her original destination. What good was the most exquisite physical connection unless two people really knew each other? Reed hadn't known about her fantasy life, about her molten core, but he had known a lot about her . . . and so, by heaven, would Doug Stewart.

Farmingdale River Inn, a red clapboard structure that had once been a private home, advertised its present status in neon. Jukebox music with a decided disco flavor dominated the summer soundscape as Laurel and Doug got out of the car.

"Why do I have a feeling," Doug said, "that we're not on your usual side of the tracks?" Their footsteps echoed loudly as they crunched across the rough stones of the parking area, and he added, "Have you actually been here before? Or were you waiting for the right disreputable stranger to accompany you?"

"If your golf shots were as accurate as your perceptions about people, Doug Stewart, you'd be the biggest duffer of them all!" Holding her blond head high, she preceded him through the doorway.

A dark, heavyset, mustached man approached them

in the dimly lit hallway. "Good evening," he greeted them, with practiced cordiality. "Are you dining with us this evening, or—" Breaking off his query, he moved a step nearer to them and unabashedly stared at Laurel's face. "Laurie, is that you?" he cried, and this time no one could doubt the genuineness of his warmth.

"None other," Laurel laughed, kissing the man on both cheeks. "Gino, you look fantastic. Business is good?"

"Booming. No matter what happens to the economy, people still need to have a good time, no? But, Laurie, you look—you look as though you found everything you ever wanted. You were always beautiful, but now you are radiant." Peering inquiringly at Doug, he said, "And this is—"

"This is Doug Stewart. A friend. Doug, this is Gino Domani."

"How do you do, Mr. Domani?" Doug said, offering his hand. "For a moment, I thought the great introducer had forgotten me."

"The great introducer?" Gino smiled knowingly. "That is some kind of family joke, no? You will dine with us, Laurie? As my guests? And catch me up on your news?"

"Thanks, Gino, another time we'd love to, but we only have time for a drink. Doug is playing in the Southern New England Classic over at Falling Water, and he's got an early curfew."

"That's why I never went in for sports myself," Gino said, patting the pronounced midriff only partially disguised by his well-cut pinstriped suit. Clapping Doug on the back, he said, "Go have your drink, and I'll see you later. Good evening," he greeted a couple who had come in behind Laurel and Doug. "Are you dining with us this evening, or do you wish the cocktail lounge?"

"So," Doug said, as they sat down at a small corner table in the lounge. "Let me guess. You used to come here as a rebellious teenager, eh, *Laurie?* I trust that Mummy and Daddums were properly *scandalized*. Red-flocked wallpaper, cheap chandeliers, a couple of traveling salesmen types at the bar, waitresses in frilly black blouses—shocking stuff, all right," he said sardonically, as his hazel eyes took stock of the room.

Before Laurel could reply, a college-age waitress came to the table for their drink orders.

"A glass of white wine for the lady, a Shirley Temple for me," Doug said crisply.

Not altogether successfully suppressing a giggle, the waitress said, "Thank you, sir," and headed back toward the bar.

"I was just about her age when I worked here," Laurel said, her fingers wandering over the big hands Doug had laid flat on the table. "My parents died when I was five—leaving debts, not a trust fund. I was raised by an aunt and uncle who scarcely had enough money to educate their own kids, let alone me. I put myself through college by working here and at a tearoom in town. So if you think I don't know about being broke, and about grinning for tips, and all the rest of it, you've got another guess coming, Doug Stewart."

Laurel wasn't sure what reaction she'd expected her revelation to elicit from Doug, but anger hadn't been on the list of possibilities.

His lips curling, the weathery planes of his face registering disapproval, he said, "Then there's even less excuse for your snobbery than I thought!"

Taking a cooling sip of the wine the waitress had set in front of her, Laurel was tempted to give Doug the telephone number of Yellow Cab in Hartford. The man kept pursuing her—only to put her down! Maybe this was the latest twist on courtship, Toronto-style, but Laurel was simply getting disheartened. "And yet," her mind whispered . . .

"And yet?" she silently retorted. But she knew the

answer, and it was more, much more, than explosive chemistry. Doug Stewart's very existence had an effect on her unlike anything else she'd ever felt. Whether he was her destroyer or her liberator, she wasn't certain, but he seemed to offer the ultimate clue to her own identity, the key to the mysterious vault where she would find instructions on how to live the rest of her life.

"Please," she implored him, putting her hands on the bowl of her stem glass and feeling the cool condensation as a kind of balm. "Won't you tell me where you got the idea that I'm a snob? Granted, I'm not the sort of person who instantly feels every stranger is her best friend—but is that all bad? Do you really think I don't value anyone on earth except moneyed Connecticut lawyers?" Guiltily she added, "I hope you realize I took off from Falling Water tonight without so much as saying good night to Webb Daniels."

"A little jealousy won't stop him from being crazy about you. Probably intensify his feelings."

"I don't want him to be crazy about me!" Recklessly she went on, "I want you to be crazy about me."

"So you can really shaft me?"

That did it for Laurel. She stood up, signaling for the check.

"Wait a minute," Doug said, standing. "This is my party, remember?"

"Some party, Mr. Stewart."

The waitress came over and announced that there wasn't any check, Mr. Domani was buying. Taking in Laurel's pearls and clearly expensive chiffon dress, she added disbelievingly, "Did you really once work here? Wear this tacky uniform blouse and everything?"

Laughing, Laurel said, "At your age, you look terrific in that blouse—you can get away with anything. Yes, I really did work here. When I went to Farmingdale College. Is that where you go?"

"No, I go to art school in Boston. My parents live

near here—this is my summer job. My name is Jeannie Keller, by the way."

"I'm—Laurie Campion. And this is Doug Stewart."

"Laurie indeed," Doug muttered, as they crossed the parking lot. "Folksiness doesn't become you, Lady Blue."

"Oh, give it a rest!" Laurel cried, getting in behind the wheel. She looked straight ahead as Doug settled into his bucket seat. Driving through the moon-drenched night with a silent intensity, she steered her thoughts away from the man sitting next to her. She concentrated on the sensation of the wind whipping her hair about, trying to become one with the powerful Mercedes as, earlier on the course, she'd tried to feel one with her clubs.

"What hotel are you staying at?" she rapped out, as she shifted down to start the ascent up Avon Mountain.

"The Hilton." As if trying to make amends for his hostility, Doug added jovially, "I have a great view of the state capital and—what's that park?"

"Bushnell Park," Laurel said icily.

"The old carousel in the park is something, eh? I could hear the music while I was getting dressed this morning. Strange how haunting calliope music always is. Alluring—but just a little bit menacing. Hartford looks like a pleasant city. Do you know Toronto?"

"I accompanied my husband on a business trip there. We—good Lord!" Laurel exclaimed, swerving. She pulled to a halt on the shoulder. "Did you see?"

"What was it, an animal?"

"Animal nothing! There's a little boy back there in the bushes!"

"A boy?" Doug echoed incredulously. "Are you sure?"

"I'm sure," Laurel snapped. "This is no place to park the car—but come on. We've got to find him."

"There aren't any houses around here, are there?" Doug peered out into the night.

"He's probably a runaway summer camper—it's happened before." Flicking on the emergency signal so the car would be visible to other drivers coming up the steep mountain road, she got out. Doug followed her down the road.

"Hello?" Laurel called. "Hello? We're friends, honey, whoever you are." She poked tentatively at the thick shrubbery that grew along the road, glad that tall, strong Doug Stewart was only inches away. "Hello? Hello?" An owl hooted, and she grabbed Doug's arm, then— disgusted with herself for betraying anxiety—let the comforting arm go. Nearing the spot where she was sure she'd spotted the child, she called out, "Let's play a game, honey. I'll count to ten, then you come out, okay? One, two, three, four—"

A grimy, tear-stained towhead who couldn't have been more than a few months older than Elsie Howard's eight-year-old twins emerged from behind the bushes. Clad only in thin summer pajamas, no socks on his sneakered feet, he was shivering convulsively. Before Laurel could make a move, Doug had whipped off his cashmere sport coat, put it around the tyke, and gathered him up in his arms.

"Hey, I bet somebody's missing you awfully hard," Doug said, rocking the boy as they started back toward the car, reminding Laurel of Doug's caring way with her when she'd been undone by the thunderstorm on the course. "What's your name?"

"You have a funny voice," the boy snuffled.

"I do, eh? That's because I come from far away. You know what? Where I come from, you would sound funny. What's your name?"

"John."

"John what?"

"I'm freezing," the boy said, through chattering teeth.

"John I'm freezing? Now there's an original name." Doug opened the passenger door of Laurel's car without loosening his grip on the boy. "In we go."

Laurel started the car, then pressed the toggle switch to close the convertible top, and turned on the heat.

"But I like the top down," the boy protested, snuggling into Doug's shoulder.

"Well, maybe another time we can take you for a ride with the top down," Laurel said, "but for now we've got to get you warm, right? What's your last name, honey? Did you run away from one of the camps around here?"

"How did you know?"

"Oh, maybe I once ran away from camp myself. Which one is it? Camp Tecumseh? The 'Y' camp? Camp ICY?"

"Are they going to real mad at me?" the boy asked.

"They may be a little mad," Laurel said, remembering her own great escape one long-ago summer, "but mostly they'll be glad to have you back safe and sound. You know what? The sooner we get you back, the less mad they'll be. So why don't you tell us your name and the name of the camp?"

"John Coover, and I ran away from Camp ICY. I hate them!" he burst out.

"You do?" Doug said. "Any special reason?"

"Because they're old meanies, that's why. There's a golf tournament, and I wanted to go to it because I'm going to be a great golfer someday, and they wouldn't let me go because they only take the senior campers."

"A golf tournament, eh? Which one?"

"The Southern New England Classic, and it's being held right near here, at Falling Water Country Club, isn't that neat? Tom Watson's there, and Lee Elder, and Jack Nicklaus—"

"And Johnny Miller, and Jerry Pate, and Doug Stewart."

"Who?" the boy said.

Roaring with laughter, Doug said, "The year you're

a rabbit, John Coover, I hope some fresh kid gives you 'who'!"

"A rabbit?" The boy's eyes widened. "Honest? You're a rabbit? You're actually in the Classic? You're a touring pro? And everything?"

"And everything," Doug laughed. "With a little help from the lady who's driving this rescue vehicle, my foursome was third low net in the pro-am event today. And I'm planning to win the Classic, Johnny boy, so no one ever again says 'who.'"

Daringly, Laurel commented, "I thought you were winning it for me." She turned into the long drive near the top of the mountain that led to Camp ICY.

"I hadn't forgotten," Doug told her, his voice warmer than she'd heard it in a while.

Unmindful of the goings on between the grownups, John was exulting over and over, "I don't believe it! A real pro! Wow! I don't believe it!"

"What kind of clubs do you play with?" Doug asked gravely.

"I have some cut-down Ben Hogans. How about you?"

"Mine were handmade by an old Scotsman who still talks about mashies and niblicks. You know what those are?"

"I think a mashie's like a pitching wedge and a niblick's for hitting out of the rough."

"Good for you! And speaking of being out of the rough," Doug said, "it looks as though we're here."

As Laurel pulled to a stop in front of the brightly lit A-frame building that served as the Camp ICY office, the director and several counselors rushed out calling "John?" True to Laurel's word, they seemed more relieved to have the boy back than angry over his running off. He looked relieved himself as the camp nurse led him forward to the infirmary, talking about hot chocolate.

Hal Gladstone, the director, and Laurel had met on

several occasions, and with Doug backing her up, Laurel did her best to convince him that a golf fan as ardent as John Coover ought to be allowed to attend the Classic. Though the director at first protested that he didn't want to reward John for running away, Laurel won him around by suggesting that he bring all the junior campers who wanted to attend and not single John out. She said that she was sure the committee would be happy to supply tickets of admission for the junior campers, as they had for the senior campers, and that she personally would like to treat all the campers to lunch.

"I suppose," she said to Doug as they drove away from the camp, "that you're going to accuse me of playing Lady Bountiful."

"Nothing of the sort," he said humbly. "I thought you were wonderful."

"I thought you were wonderful, too," she murmured.

"Can we go look at the moon together someplace?" Doug asked.

"There's an overlook about five minutes away from here," Laurel answered. "Do you think we'll still find each other wonderful five minutes from now?"

"Maybe if we don't say a word to each other, the feeling will hold, eh?"

Smiling her assent, Laurel turned on the radio, tuning in a college station that broadcast traditional jazz around the clock. Duke Ellington and Johnny Hodges were playing "Let's Fall in Love," a favorite version of one of her favorite songs, and she was dying to ask Doug if he knew it and cared for it, too, but she didn't dare break the pact. Pulling into a parking space in the overlook, Laurel stared at the twinkling lights of downtown Hartford and the bright summer moon. Was she really there with Doug, or was she in the velvet grip of another fantasy? Like the Doug she had conjured in her mind, he let an exquisite tension build up between them, then, like the Doug of her fantasy but a thousand times more compelling, he pulled her out from behind the steering wheel and brought his lips down on hers. Their kiss frantically escalated as they tasted each other and had to have more.

"Laurel," he whispered urgently, his mouth traveling over her face, catching at an earlobe, brushing tenderly across her eyelids. "Laurel, Laurel."

She gave herself over to a giddy joy as his fingers explored the hollows around her collarbone, then teased the eager swell of her breasts. He rubbed the chiffon of her dress against her stiffening nipples, reaching behind her to release the zipper so he could lower her bodice and put his mouth where his hands had been.

Laurel's fingers danced wildly through his long sandy hair, her hands guiding the motions of his head, urging his lips to close on her flesh there...there...there. Doug pulled back, and Laurel's heart lurched with the fear that she had once again managed to displease him, but he let her know he merely wanted space between them so his eyes could discover the pulsing beauty his lips had been celebrating.

"So many shades of pink," he murmured tenderly, a gentle finger tracing a path around one aureole, then advancing to the deeper cerise of a nipple. He leaned forward again to visit soft kisses on the faint line her clinging bodice had left on her skin, then he moved away once more, leaning against the car door, so he could watch his hands make a teasing assault on her breasts. He lifted his hazel eyes to take in the way Laurel's own blue eyes roamed eagerly from his face to his hands on her skin and back to his face.

"I want to make love to you in front of a mirror," he said hoarsely. "I want to watch you watching me as I take off all your clothes and make love to every inch of your body. Does that shock you?"

Unable to speak, Laurel shook her blond head, offering her breasts up to him yet again. "Everything," she finally whispered.

"Then come to my hotel with me," Doug said. "Now. I don't think I can wait much longer."

Laurel's breath caught in her throat. She wanted him so much, but a hotel in downtown Hartford? Where she was sure to be seen by other people involved in the Classic, people who knew her and Dean, and had known Reed? Unconsciously she reached for her bodice, pulling it up over her exposed skin. If she said no, would she be subjected to another tirade about her values? But, damn it, there was nothing wrong with caring about one's self-respect. There was nothing admirable about being scandalous. "I can't," she said. "I want you, but not like that. I'd feel cheap." Instantly she regretted the word, but too late.

"I see," Doug said gratingly. "Lady Blue doesn't go to hotels. Because what *they* think is more important than what *we* feel, eh?"

"Please," she tried. "Please. It's been so wonderful—"

"Hasn't it just? But everything wonderful has to stop before it gets out of control—that's the rule, isn't it? As long as we're in *your* car, or in *your* Mrs. Epstein's barn, fine. Indulge the senses a little—what the hell? It's good for the complexion—everyone knows that." He leaned back against the maroon leather headrest and folded his arms. "All right, then, Lady Blue. Take me home to your bed. What could be a safer place?"

"I can't!" Laurel cried. "I share my home with a sensitive seventeen-year-old boy."

"Like I said, I'm sure he knows all about kissing. And the rest. Do you think it's somehow healthier for him to think that your body ceased to have life when his father's did?"

"Please, Doug, please. How could you be so attuned to a child like little John yet so brutal about another child's feelings a few minutes later?"

"Seventeen isn't a child. At seventeen, I—"

"I don't want to hear about it!" Laurel exclaimed. "I know Dean, and you don't, and all I can tell you is that he's worried enough about you as it is, without my bringing you home and waving you under his nose."

"Worried about me, eh? Doesn't think the old Canadian jock is a worthy successor to his dad? Or maybe he's rooting for that lawyer friend of yours."

Laurel gritted her teeth. If ever a man had a genius for getting things backwards, it was Doug Stewart. She moved back behind the steering wheel and got the car going.

"Look," Doug said, as they started down the mountain in the direction of Hartford, "I don't want you to think I really did want to wave sex under Dean's nose. I thought we could all hang out together, talk about the event today—then, when he went to sleep, you and I could move on to other things."

"What do you think," Laurel said, "that he's a little kid who has milk and cookies at nine and then goes to sleep with a teddy bear? He's usually up listening to his music after I've gone to bed."

"Well, well!" Doug said triumphantly. "So you admit he's not a little kid!"

"Doug Stewart, you are absolutely, postively the most infuriating man I have ever encountered, and I'm dropping you off at your hotel, and I don't want to hear another word about it!"

"Yes, m'lady," Doug said, with a meekness that surprised her but didn't make her change her mind. "Would you mind putting the top down again? I know you've got a built-in cooling system, but I'm hot as the dickens."

Laurel put the top down. They drove the rest of the way in silence.

"Thanks for the ride," Doug said, as Laurel pulled into the circular drive in front of the tall blue glass facade of the Hartford Hilton. Then, softly laying fingers against Laurel's cheek, he said, "You will be in my gallery tomorrow, won't you? I can't get the equation out of my mind—if I win the Classic, I'll win you."

"I do want you to win, Doug," Laurel said enigmatically. "I'll be there tomorrow." Dropping a fleeting kiss on his lips, she took off.

chapter

6

SUDDENLY EXHAUSTED IN body and spirit, Laurel decided that speed mattered more at the moment than scen-
ery. She got on the major east-west artery, Route 84,
instead of the older, prettier, but decidedly slower roads
she generally preferred. Though she had no covering
over her thin dress, and the air had a definite nip to it
as she zipped along toward Farmingdale and home, she
kept the top of the Mercedes down because she knew she
needed every lungful of oxygen so she could simply stay
awake.

By the time she was tucking the car away in the garage
next to Dean's cherished vintage Ford station wagon, she
felt as though her body had been bludgeoned. Her temples were pounding painfully, and her mouth was desert
dry—unmistakable signals that a head cold—or, worse,

the flu—was on its way. Determined to bribe her body back to robustness, she went to the kitchen to make tea. A note in Dean's handwriting was propped against the sugar bowl, and she eagerly snatched it up—hoping against all reason that it would tell her Doug had called during the last half hour and was waiting by his hotel-room telephone, penitent and eager.

"Dear Laurel," the note read, "that new pasta is great. I left some steak in the fridge in case you come home hungry—I know they never feed you anything serious at those cocktail buffets. Don't be nervous if my light is off—I got really wiped out today. I checked with the club and Doug is teeing off at nine-thirty. I set my alarm so I can bring you breakfast in bed at eight. Please write your order below. Anything fancy at your own risk! Love, Dean."

As she put the note down, tears filled Laurel's eyes. Dean had demons to wrestle with, but at heart he was every bit as sweet as his father had been. If only he could find some direction, some ambition to make him want to get up and get going *every* morning.

Her thoughts turned, as they often did at such moments, to Dean's absentee mother. Did she ever wonder about the nature of the boy she had abandoned in infancy; did she feel a pang on his birthdays, silently size up blond teenage boys on the street and wonder if they could be Dean? Whatever success Eleanor Campion had achieved with her painting, whatever emotional fulfillment she'd found in the south of France, did it remotely make up for the loss of a child? Sighing for all the complexities of life, Laurel got the electric kettle going and took down a tin of chamomile tea.

"Children...children," she murmured, halving a lemon and opening a jar of local honey. Doug Stewart had looked as much at home with a grimy boy in his arms as he did with his handmade golf clubs in his grip. Laurel felt a little flutter of panic at the back of her throat as she wondered where Doug had learned about small boys. He had never been married, he'd told her, but he had loved. With his apparent delight in flouting convention, had he fathered a child out of wedlock? Laurel found herself in the grip of a cold dread at the thought that another woman and child might have first call on him.

"You *must* have the flu," she said aloud, as yet another fantasy floated to the forefront of her mind. Only this fantasy wasn't sensual at all—it was homey as muffins, and it involved a happy threesome of Doug, Laurel, and Dean playing all the great golf courses of the world because the family that played together stayed together—

The sound of the kettle at full boil brought her back to the vicinity of reality. While the tea steeped, she found a pencil and wrote on the back of Dean's note.

"Dear Room Service," she scrawled. "and it isn't even Mother's Day! Orange juice, toast, and coffee would be much appreciated. In case the chef hasn't been informed, please tell him that there's a new Elsie Howard home-made cracked wheat bread in the refrigerator that should make great toast. P.S. Thanks for leaving the kitchen neater than you found it. Love, Laurel."

As she put the note where he'd left his for her, Laurel looked at the clock. Only eleven-thirty, but she felt as if it were four in the morning. Lord, maybe she was getting old . . . too old to have a child. Then again, Elsie Howard was thirty-five, and Pete, her husband, who was a physician, was pressing her to have another child. . . .

Shaking her head, feeling as though her mind was chasing her around the kitchen, Laurel hastily put the teapot, lemon, honey, a cup, a napkin, and a spoon on a small silver tray, and started upstairs. Her mischievous thoughts went right upstairs with her. Thirty-two really wasn't too old to have a child, especially if you were an athlete and in good shape. Genuinely maternal as her feelings were toward Dean, she'd always felt a bit cheated that she'd never held a newborn, never nursed, never had the gratification of seeing her eyes or hair or way of walking or a trick of speech get a new lease on life in a child. Reed had never ruled out having a child with Laurel, but he'd kept pushing back the date when he wanted to talk about it, much less do something about it, and Laurel had realized he had deep misgivings about becoming a father again in his fifties. When he'd died, she'd had a brief, wild hope that they'd outwitted the mechanics of birth control and she was carrying his child, but of course she hadn't been. Since then, the subject had been far from her conscious mind.

In the few hours since she'd met Doug, though, it seemed as though every possible question had presented itself to Laurel—and no answers! Putting on a lacy blue nightgown that tied under her breasts, she got into bed, doctored a cup of tea, leaned back against heaped-up pillows, and sipped, trying to fathom the man's effect on her. Hopeless. She might as well try to understand the intricacies of space flight.

Turning off the light, she slipped into a never-never-land in which she and Doug were wandering in a field of giant cabbages, and each cabbage had a sandy-haired baby in it waiting to be born, and all she and Doug had to do to get a baby was make love in the shade of a cabbage, and soon they had dozens of children. . . .

"Room service!" a cheery voice said.

Peeling her eyes open, Laurel looked balefully at a brightly smiling Dean, holding a breakfast tray in his hands.

"But I haven't even gone to sleep yet," she groaned, as Dean released the folding legs and propped the tray on her bed. She tried to pull herself up to a sitting position, but it seemed to be a physical demand her body couldn't meet. The wholesome smell of Elsie's home-made bread, freshly toasted, nauseated her. The front page of the *Hartford Courant,* which Dean had folded and propped against the coffee pot, swam in front of her eyes.

"Are you okay, Laurel?" Dean asked. Unlike him, Laurel was usually a morning person.

Weakly she shook her head, "I'm afraid I'm sick, damn it." Thinking about Dean looking forward to walking the course with her, and Doug playing his qualifying round, and little John Coover and his friends coming to Falling Water as her guests, she wailed, "I can't be sick, I refuse." She managed to sit upright and reached for a glass of orange juice. That slight effort seemed, oh unfair world, to reverberate painfully in her temples. The icy sensation imparted by the juice glass made her realize how warm her body was. "I refuse to have a fever," she defiantly told Dean, as he fetched a thermometer from the bathroom. But, knowing her body as well as she did, she was well aware that her temperature was over a hundred even before she consulted the mercury.

"Dean, I'm so sorry, your lovely breakfast, but I don't think—oh, gosh, you even went outside and got a rose. You're a darling. But I don't think—"

"I understand," he said, bending for the tray.

"But would you leave the rose on my bedside table? Oh, that looks so nice. I've got to call Pete Howard and see if he can stop by and give me some magical pill that will fix me up. And I've got to get Elsie to take care of John Coover—"

"Who?"

"A runaway we found on Avon Mountain. No, I'm not delirious with fever, I'll tell you later." She looked at Dean as she reached for her blue bedside phone and started to dial Elsie's number. "How are *you*, sweetie? Feeling less wiped out after a good night's sleep?"

"I feel great," Dean said.

Sticking out her tongue, Laurel said, "If I didn't love you, I'd hate you, I'm so jealous. Did you ever have the sort of headache," she groaned, "that hurt worse when you dialed the telephone? I—Pete? Hi. I'm glad I got you before you left for the office. Help! I need a body transplant!"

Twenty minutes later Pete Howard was in her bedroom in person, poking her with the kind of offhand thoroughness she'd come to respect deeply, asking the usual rude questions.

"What do I have?" she asked in return. "And to whom can I give, lend, or sell it?"

"Well, your respiratory tract is clear, and aside from that slight nausea, there's nothing wrong with your gut—" Tossing a used tongue depressor into a wastebasket, he grinned and said, "If I didn't know you better, I'd say you were either hung over or having morning sickness."

"Hung over on four sips of wine?" Laurel said indignantly. "As for the second diagnosis, doctor, if I'm pregnant, I'm going to make medical history! And for your information, if and when I *am* pregnant, I'm not going to have morning sickness. I don't believe in morning-sickness."

"And what Laurel Campion doesn't believe in, she doesn't have." Pete sat on the edge of Laurel's bed. "I didn't even dare suggest you might have some kind of allergy. I know you don't believe in allergies."

"Seriously, Pete, is it flu? I've got to get out to Falling Water this morning."

"It's not flu. I'd say it's a mixture of the aftereffects of your exposure yesterday—and, though I know Laurel Campion doesn't have a psyche, is there maybe something big on your mind? Just an educated guess, but I get the feeling your body wants to ground you for a day or so."

Laurel stuck out her tongue at him, but she didn't marshal her usual arguments against anything but the most cut and dried diagnosis. "Leaving aside what it is, how do I get rid of it?"

"Aspirin and plenty of fluids for your headache and fever—and I heartily recommend that you follow the signals you're getting and just hang around your bed for a day or so. Take the aspirin with milk to make it easier on your gut. Call me at the office at noon if the fever isn't down." Washing up in the bathroom, he called out cheerfully over the sound of running water, "That Doug Stewart's an interesting fellow. I'd say you'd met your match, Laurel." He was off with a cheerful wave before Laurel could reply.

Bringing her aspirin and a goblet of ice-cold milk, Dean said, "Gee, Laurel, this is almost fun. I never get a chance to take care of you."

"Oh, shut up," she murmured, but affectionately, swallowing the aspirin and willing that it make her instantly well. Then she added curiously, "Is that really what I project, Dean? Someone who never gets sick . . . never needs anything?"

His delicate features furrowing as he considered the question, he said, "Well, you've hardly ever asked for my help. I mean, sometimes you ask me to do things around the house because you think I should do them, but never because you think *you* can't do them. You're a real take-charge lady. You always seem to know what you want and how to get it. That's why you win on the golf course, isn't it? Dad always said he was a topflight golfer because he knew how to use his body—and you were topflight because you knew how to use your mind."

Leaning back into her pillows, Laurel thought about his words, but thinking seemed to make her temples pound harder. A groan escaped from between her lips.

Hesitantly, Dean said, "I know a headache cure that might work faster than aspirin."

Laurel cocked one eye. "Some mystical nonsense?" One of the sources of tension in the Campion household was Dean's belief that nearly any "alternative" remedy for the ills of body, spirit, nation, and planet was apt to prove more reliable than the conventional remedy.

"Nothing mystical about it," Dean said defensively. "It's just Eastern instead of Western, that's all. You don't think acupuncture is mumbo jumbo, do you?"

"I suppose not," Laurel conceded. "But I'll thank you not to turn me into a pincushion. My Western body responds better to Western medicine."

"My cure is acupressure, which is the same system as acupuncture, only you apply pressure to different points on your body instead of sticking in needles. To cure a headache, you press your temples, and your wrists, and the back of the neck. Like this," he said, demonstrating on himself. "Want to try? It can't hurt."

Following his instructions, Laurel conceded that the throbbing in her head was diminishing—but, then again, maybe the aspirin was doing its work. In any event, she still didn't feel capable of walking more than the few yards to her bathroom and back to her bed. The unsinkable Laurel Campion just wasn't going to make it to Falling Water in time to see Doug tee off for the day's round. She asked Dean to take her place in Doug's gallery and explain her absence when he could get Doug's ear. She called Elsie and asked her friend to make arrangements at the club for the ICY junior campers to be admitted to the Classic and to have lunch as Laurel's treat.

She stayed awake long enough to hear Dean's car take off, then sank into a hot, restless sleep in which cabbages kept turning into golf balls and Dean was a runaway camper from ICY and her Aunt Bett and Uncle Jack wanted to sell the condominium she'd bought for them in Florida and move back to Windsor . . . only the house in Windsor was really Webb Daniel's blue saltbox, and Doug wouldn't let her go inside . . . he simply put his arms around her and crushed her breasts against his chest—

The ringing of the telephone penetrated her dream state.

"Hello?" she said thickly.

"Hello, Laurel, it's Sara," she heard her sister-in-law say through a thick fog that seemed to separate them. "I wanted to catch you before you left for the club."

"Not going to the club," Laurel managed to get out. "Sick."

"Oh, are you, dear? I'm sorry to hear that. I suppose it was that skimpy dress in the air-conditioned clubhouse. Really, Laurel, I—"

"Sara, I hate to be rude, but this is the first time I've been sick since I was ten and had chicken pox, so if I could just be allowed to wallow in peace—"

"I have news, dear, that I know you'll want to hear before anyone else does," Sara said.

Even in her fogbound condition, Laurel realized that Sara had called her "dear" twice in five minutes, and that her voice had a strange, sugary quality to it—even if she hadn't been able to resist jibing at Laurel's chiffon dress. Alarm bells went off in Laurel's mind. She forced herself to sit up and took a sip of the ice water that Dean had thoughtfully left on her bedside table, next to the white rose he'd picked for her. "What's the news, Sara?" she asked, in a voice that somewhat resembled its normal crispness.

"Eleanor Ligeret is coming to town."

"Who?"

"Oh, of course," Sara said. "You still think of her as Eleanor Campion. She remarried several years ago. A French art dealer who has both inherited wealth and—"

"She wants to see Dean?" Laurel interrupted. The shock of the news that Dean's mother was coming to Farmingdale had the perverse effect of sweeping the pain from her head and jolting her into full alertness.

"She wants to take Dean," Sara said, in a voice Laurel couldn't quite read. She sounded anxious, yet strangely excited in a spiteful kind of way.

"Take him? But she can't. She surrendered custody when she and Reed got their divorce. And now I'm his legal guardian."

"But he turns eighteen next month, dear. Then the choice is his. Perhaps he'll like the idea of living with his natural mother and a man who is much more appropriate a stepfather than—"

"Than whom?" Laurel interjected into the pause Sara had left. Suspicions danced around the edge of her mind, but she decided they were unworthy—the product of her fevered state—and she did her best to ignore them.

"Well, than another sort of man Eleanor might well have fallen for, An artist, say."

"I thought you said her husband was an art dealer."

"Well, yes, dear. But that's very different, isn't it? Besides, I believe he comes from one of the great noble families of Burgundy, though he doesn't use his title."

"Oh, Lord," Laurel groaned, not caring for the moment that she was letting her guard down in front of Sara. She found herself reaching for a cigarette—though she had quit smoking the night Reed had proposed to her, six years ago. A part of her mind told her not to worry, she had powerhouse lawyer Webb Daniels on her side, but another part of her mind realized that the heart, not the law, was going to be the final arbiter here—and who could predict the heart?

As Sara jabbered on about the details of Eleanor's flights from Paris to New York, and New York to Bradley International, the airport serving northern Connecticut and western Massachusetts, Laurel kept hearing unnerving undertones in Sara's voice that made it hard to concentrate on her words. Lying on her pillows after she'd hung up, her eyes darting around her blue room, she found one thought, one wish, surfacing in her mind. If only Doug Stewart were her ally, not her enemy! Then she could do anything! She really could be that slightly larger-than-life take-charge lady Dean saw her as, because she knew it was imperative to make the right moves now.

Laurel looked at the small clock on her bedside table. Doug would be just about ready to tee off. Were those judgmental eyes of his sweeping the crowd, all too ready to mark her "not present"? Was he gloating at her defection, inventing harsh stories in his mind to cover his hurt? Because he *would* be hurting. For all his sneers and snarls, he was quick as a child to be stung, Laurel knew. Come to think of it, he did most of his sneering and snarling precisely when he'd been stung by real or imagined wasps. Oh, Lord, if he didn't play well today, he would blame her—she was certain of it. But if he did play well, without her there, that would be painful for her in a way too. Laurel's eyelids grew heavy, and she sank under their weight, grateful to be relieved of the responsiblity of running the whole world.

In her dreams her fever consumed her because the fever was named Doug Stewart, and he'd crept into the house, stripped off his clothes, and taken his rightful place beside her in bed. His hands were gentle as they slid up and down the silken slopes of her nightgown, and she knew he didn't want her to wake up, that he wanted to merge with her in the tranquil blue pools of her dreaming mind, where she was able to let go. "Float," he was whispering in her ear. Or was it "flood?" Or was it "love?" Whatever the word, it was the right word, and his breath was the right breath, and his touch was the right touch.

She wanted to wake up and be with him for real and respond to him but a voice warned her that if she woke up, she would have to send him away on the grounds that the bed was Reed's bed. But it *wasn't* Reed's bed because her body wasn't Reed's body. Had been, had been...but wasn't now. "Love again," Reed had told her, and he'd meant those words. If what they'd had was real, then nothing could undo it. It had been real, had been love, and Doug was real, was love—

She woke up, raging with thirst. The water beside her bed had gone tepid, and she decided nothing but mineral water in a glass piled high with ice cubes would do. Throwing a matching blue silk peignoir over her nightgown, she began the perilous trip downstairs. What an extraordinary thing the human body was—one day energetically tramping the fairways, the next day all but undone by a mere flight of stairs. But the trip had been worth it, she decided, as she stood by the kitchen window, staring out at the rich blue green of the spruces that flanked her driveway like so many sentinels. She downed one icy glass of mineral water, then another, and for the first time since awakening to Dean's unwelcome breakfast tray, felt something like human.

As she saw Dean's car turn into the driveway, her heart gave a little lurch. She wasn't yet by any means in shape to break the news to him about his mother's impending visit. Would there ever be a good moment? Better to get it over with as soon as possible, she decided grimly. She thought about freshening up in the downstairs powder room before Dean got inside, then decided not to. Dean had seemed to take some measure of comfort in the discovery that Laurel, too, had her moments of being undone, of needing him. Maybe in the inevitably emotional discussion to come it would help him to see Laurel without any armor on at all—not even lipstick.

But—good Lord—Doug Stewart was in the car with Dean! Well—so be it. Cynic that he was, he'd probably only half believed Dean's explanation of Laurel's absence at Falling Water that morning. One glimpse of her now and he'd know the truth beyond a shadow of a doubt. Dean *could* have called and warned her, *should* have called and warned her—but this was no time for her to scold him, and she would let the breach pass.

"I tried to call," were Dean's first words, "but the phone was constantly busy. I thought maybe you'd taken it off the hook so you could get some sleep. We were going to make a really quiet entrance just in case. Anyway, Mr. Stewart has some news."

"Where are you going?" Laurel called after him, as he started for the door.

"I told your little pal John that I'd come back and give him and some of the other campers a putting lesson. Gee, you don't think Mr. Newfield will mind, do you?"

"I think he'll survive." Laurel suppressed a smile at the notion that the club pro would consider Dean competition in the teaching business. "Did you have lunch?"

"Yes, Mother." Then, grinning an apology for his teenage sarcasm, Dean hurriedly asked, "You feeling better? You look better. At least you have some color in your cheeks. You need anything from the drugstore?"

"I'm fine, thanks, sweetie."

"Don't drive Mr. Stewart anywhere," Dean ordered, in a proprietary voice that made Laurel do battle with her emotions. "I'll be back in a couple of hours. Around three," he said, as if Laurel couldn't, in her present condition, add two hours to one o'clock and come up with three o'clock. "Or he can call a cab."

"You seem to have a thing for bossy men," Doug said, as the door closed behind Dean.

Laurel mused for a moment, then said, "In his case, it's brand-new. And I have to admit, I find it rather charming—in his case." Taking stock of the light in Doug's eyes, a glow to his deeply tanned face, she said delightedly, "It looks to me as though you didn't have any trouble qualifying this morning. You definitely have the air of a man who made the cut."

"Six under par," Doug said, with no pretense whatsoever at modesty.

"Fantastic!"

"The funny thing is," Doug said, "it was a very uneven round. I was two over at the turn—and then that very smart stepson of yours got kind of aggressive with me and let me know why my muse wasn't in my gallery. I proceeded to get eight birdies in a row, then merely shot par on the eighteenth."

Leaning against the cool stainless steel of the sink, Laurel shook her head disbelievingly and said, "You really could end up winning the Classic!"

"What did I tell you I came to town to do? Among other things."

Laurel stood looking at him in a happy daze, her eyes feasting on his sandy hair, still dewy from a shower, and the extraordinary vitality and complex intelligence that radiated from his hazel eyes. The crisp, tattersall shirt he wore was open two buttons, revealing a luxurious sprinkling of tightly curled hair on his chest. Today's jeans were every bit as disreputable as the pair he'd worn the day before, but today Laurel couldn't help noticing that the faded denim did a rather splendid job of displaying the rippling muscles of the man's thighs.

Clapping her hand to her mouth, she said, "What am I thinking of? Can I get you a drink? I know you're in training, but maybe some mineral water? Iced tea?"

"How about a Shirley Temple?" he teased. "You are a stickler for the proprieties, Lady Blue. Never mind that you'd be in a heap if it weren't for that sink holding you up. I've been trying all morning to get Dean to call me Doug, but you've got this 'mister' business drummed into his head so tightly, his tongue kind of gets stuck when he tries 'Doug.' Anyway, nothing to drink, thanks. I had a Coke with little John and his friends."

"Is John having fun?" Laurel asked, trying hard not think about cabbages.

"It's merely the best day of his life. Now you should be back in bed, eh?"

"Is that an order, doctor?"

Looking startled for an instant, then grinning, he said, "Absolutely. And, knowing the patient's tendencies toward insubordination, I think I'd better come upstairs and enforce it. Pretty house," he said, as they walked down a hallway that offered glimpses of the dining room and living room. "Is that a Degas?" he asked, pointing to an oil of two young dancers putting on their ballet slippers.

"It is. Do you like it?"

"I admire it—but I can't say it excites me. I'd probably trade it in for some Eskimo pieces, and maybe an oil by Riopelle—he's an angry French-Canadian—and some wild, experimental stuff from New York. You're surprised I care about paintings, eh?"

"Doug Stewart, the only thing that will ever surprise me about you is if you are unsurprising two minutes in a row. Did you grow up with art?" she asked, as they started up the stairs.

"Me? I grew up in a caddy shack."

"Oh, stop," she scolded. "You're probably the black sheep son of some wealthy Canadian industrialist who would regard this house as a vacation cottage."

"Is that what you want to think?" Doug asked, his voice ominously quiet.

Stumbling as she turned to give him a chiding look, Laurel would have tripped on a step if Doug hadn't caught hold of her arm. A tremor ran through her body, and she knew it had nothing to do with the slight fever she was still running. "Were there ever two people who found more things to fight about?" she asked, with a wistful little sigh.

"It's something to do between kisses," Doug grinned.

"Maybe we should take up chess," Laurel said, standing at the top of the stairs.

"Maybe we shouldn't allow so much time between kisses." Putting gentle hands on her shoulders, he let his lips graze hers in a teasing assault that left her ravenous for more.

"Do I taste awful?" she said.

"You taste like morning. The way you'd taste if we

were married and truly got to know each other. Delicious, really." Giving his words emphasis, he let his tongue flick lazily at the corners of her mouth, then he forced her lips open as he sought another taste. "Nectar," he murmured. "And you look like morning, with your hair all mussed and your face bare. God, woman, I want to know you every way, everywhere, in dark country fields and on the bright streets of cities at noontime; I want to make love to you on trains and planes and all the haylofts of Connecticut and hotel rooms and in bathtubs—" He stopped dead still, peering intently at her face, a glint of amusement in his eyes. "That isn't a faint bit of blush on the Campion cheek, is it?"

"Certainly not," Laurel said coolly.

"Bathtubs are taking it a step too far, eh?"

"I repeat, certainly not. You carry on as if you were some missionary of sensuality from a hot, sultry land, bringing the true word to icebound old Connecticut."

"Then you've made love in a bathtub?" Doug said gravely.

"Well, not exactly," Laurel began. "But I've thought about it. I've thought about doing it with you, if you must know—so there. And have you made love in many bathtubs?" she mimicked.

"Well, not exactly," he mimicked in return. "But I'm thinking about it. With you. Is there indoor plumbing in this establishment?"

Laurel took him by the hand, led him through her bedroom into the master bath, and pointed out the gleaming double-size whirlpool bath.

Letting out a loud whistle, Doug said, "You mean you own this splendid playground and you haven't done anything except take baths in it?"

"Are you sorry I waited for you?" Laurel asked gravely.

"Oh, Lord, no!" he exclaimed, hugging her to him, hands caressing her hair, mouth fixing on hers.

A small, blissful eternity later, Laurel disengaged herself to turn on the water taps, her fever long forgotten. She opened a linen closet next to the sink, sending the scent of violets into the bathroom, and took out an armful of thick blue towels and washcloths.

"Someone once told me blue was the color of frigidity," Doug murmured, "and I was fool enough to believe him. Can I help?"

"You could take off your clothes."

Feigning shock, he said, "You mean you bathe naked in Connecticut? I thought that was against the blue laws."

"Lady Blue has her own blue laws," Laurel said, with a little smile. "Do you want scent in the water? I have some salts that smell like the sea."

"Sounds nice." As she threw a capful under the water cascading into the steaming tub, he added, "I ought to warn you, I have mermaid fantasies. Can you grow a tail on demand?"

"No," Laurel said, "but I can bark like a sea lion. Does that turn you on?"

"Coming from you, Lady B, it just might." He unbuttoned his shirt and laid it on the back of a blue and gold vanity chair. Under Laurel's watchful eyes, he took off his leather sneakers and socks, then let his hands stray to his belt.

"You're a beautiful man, Doug Stewart," Laurel said softly, her eyes drinking in his superb musculature, the exciting lines of demarcation between his natural, fair skin and the deep tan he'd earned on the course. "Be naked for me." Smiling, he took off his jeans, and she stood there watching, rooted in a pure, aesthetic appreciation of his animal grace. Though he was naked and she was clothed, his beauty and his self-assuredness made her feel that she was at his mercy . . . and she wouldn't have had it any other way.

She reached up to take off her peignoir, but Doug signaled that he wanted to undress her, and she complaisantly dropped her hands and let his fingers work her bows and hooks and snaps. Then she too stood naked, and she proudly noted that he took as much pleasure in her beauty as she took in his.

"Turn around," he commanded gently, and she un-self-consciously pirouetted, letting him glimpse her body from every angle. "Now that's a magnificent work of art," he commented. Reaching over, he let his fingers trickle casually between her breasts, bringing her close to convulsions of delight and expectation.

"Bath, anyone?" she asked. Bending over to test the temperature of the water, she got a playful spank on one buttock, leading to an indignantly uttered "Doug Stewart!", leading to a kiss so heated that she began to grow faint in Doug's arms.

With utmost tenderness, he lowered her into the sweet, briny water, quickly following her.

"Lord," Laurel murmured, "I hope this doesn't do me in. Not that sharing a tub with you isn't worth dying for."

"Actually, it's just what the doctor ordered. A tepid tub brings the fever right down. And then," he said, with a smile she found deliciously evil, "I have a plan for bringing your fever right back up."

Suddenly their mood turned playful, and they went at each other with a kind of savage innocence, teasing each other with soap and washcloths, splashing tender flesh, then apologizing with kisses. As Doug's strong, deft hands lathered her breasts, then sluiced them with clear water, Laurel thought in happy abandon that being afloat with him in their private sea was sweeter than the most splendidly embroidered of her solitary fantasies.

She activated the water jets, and they lolled in sensual abandon in each other's arms as the powerful spray caressed them and heightened their arousal.

"Laurel," Doug groaned, "I have to have you, and I

think it better be on dry land or we're both going to drown."

"Yes, my captain," she murmured, convinced that he could ask nothing of her that wouldn't dovetail with her own desires.

Quickly toweling each other dry, they moved from bath to bedroom.

Laurel pushed her pillow away and lay flat on the mattress, arching toward Doug, offering him her long, taut throat, signaling to him that she was at his mercy— willingly. Nipping gently at her throat to answer that he was staking claim to her, he then buried his face in her hair, offering her the softest of kisses, moaning his complicity and pleasure when she nibbled softly at an earlobe, then teased him with her tongue until he ordered her to stop, lest he explode.

"Explode, explode," she begged him. "I'm too greedy for you to wait. Take me, darling—and later we can go back and do it by the book."

"My love!" he cried, as they swelled and peaked together, Laurel crying out his name over and again.

As her passion subsided and gave way to a glow reaching as far as her small toes, she murmured, "I do believe you just set a new course record." She made a pillow of his arm, and with his words of affection and praise as her lullaby, fell quickly asleep.

chapter

7

AS IF THEY had shared a bed for all eternity, Laurel awoke groping for Doug. Encountering only a pillow and tangled bed linen, she sighed her disappointment and tried to conjure a dream that would restore him to her. But her body let her know it had had enough of lolling about, thank you, and she opened her eyes.

The white rose Dean had given her that morning had begun to unfold, perfuming the room. Even more beautiful to her eyes was the sight of a note under the slender silver vase in a bold hand that could only be Doug's.

"Dearest," she read, "I know how sensitive you are about Dean, and rightly! So I'm reluctantly abandoning you while the coast is clear. I'll walk to Farmingdale Center and get a cab to the hotel from there. If you wake up feeling as glorious as you look right now, want to show me the local sights? Not that I could see anything more appealing than what I got to look at today, you luscious, shameless creature! I thought maybe we could drive to the shore for lobster later—think Dean and his red-haired girl would like to double-date with a couple of old fogies? Of if you'd rather just be a twosome, drop the word in your humble slave's ear. By the way, you'd apparently knocked the phone off the hook in your sleep this morning, which is why Dean couldn't reach you when he tried to call—and I left it off so you could sleep. I adore, you, Lady Blue. XXX, Doug."

Reading it over and over, glad that no one was there to witness her silly, teenage behavior, Laurel basked in the tenderness Doug had conveyed. Did she dare to believe that the real Doug had written this note—and the cynical, tough-tempered Doug was a phantom who'd melted into the air? Not that she'd want all his edges to be smoothed, she forced herself to admit. His teasing comments earlier notwithstanding, she didn't really want a life full of bossy men—but she didn't want to be anybody's boss, either. A meeting of strengths was what appealed to her, whether the relationship was the one between her and Dean, or her and Elsie, or her and— did she dare think of him this way?—a new lover.

Letting her fingers playfully stroke the skin he had repeatedly caressed to fever pitch, she wondered if the act of love really had been love for Doug. Lord knows he'd poured reckless words of tenderness into her ears, hinting at a never-ending future of intimacy, but she was well aware that only a fool gave full credence to utterances made between the sheets. If she just knew more about him, were better able to weigh and sort his actions! In a sense she felt she knew everything that really mattered about him because her every instinct had told her he had character, even if he seemed to go out of his way to conceal it. Then again, she knew so few *facts* about him. She'd been frankly afraid to ask,even the routine

questions about his parents and education and what kind
of house or apartment he lived in now and what he ate
for breakfast. He was all too likely to interpret any question as a manifestation of her snobbish anxieties—as
witness his reaction to her question about whether he'd
grown up with art on the walls. She didn't even know
which of the Toronto clubs he played out of, and whether
he'd been a teaching pro before he qualified for the tour.
Heaven help her if she brought up the loaded question
of country clubs!

She loved the idea of a double date that evening with
Dean and Ginny Demerest, and the kids would be thrilled
to pieces. But she was now determined to risk asking
Doug questions, and for that one reason was sorry they
wouldn't be alone at dinner. Had Doug in fact proposed
the double date because he wanted to postpone telling
his story? No, she decided—that was an unfair thought.
He'd asked her to show him the sights of Hartford, after
all, and there would be plenty of lulls in the historical
and architectural discussions in which to get a little personal.

Swinging her legs out of bed, testing the floor and
finding to her delight that it didn't wobble, Laurel wondered for an uneasy moment if Doug hadn't put his finger
on a slightly unpleasant truth about her. Was her curiosity
about his background and lifestyle as disinterested as she
wanted to think it was? Or had there been a kind of
nervous wishful thinking in her earlier joke about his
being the black sheep son of a wealthy family? She knew
that wealth didn't make people better—but she knew it
didn't necessarily make them any worse, and if she were
going to be absolutely honest with herself, she supposed
she would be happier than not if he turned out to have
more than the chancy income of the touring golfer. But,
damn it, there was only one reason she cared, and no
one could call it a venal one. She had a great deal of
money, left to her by Reed, and money was power—and

she didn't want to have more power than the man she loved. No way, though, was she going to let the question of money come between them. She could live without things, but she wasn't sure she could live without Doug. If she had to divest herself of her wealth to make the relationship work, she would.

The man she loved. The unspoken phrase seemed to reverberate throughout the blue room, as though it were the incantation of a thundering chorus.

Was she making more of sex than she should? She grilled herself as she stood at the bathroom sink, splashing cold water on her face; she probed every last corner of her mind in search of truth. Was she simply trying to justify the sublime excesses of physical union with Doug? No, she decided resoundingly. Gorgeous though their lovemaking had been, it had echoed, not invented, the emotions already there in her heart, challenging her to recognize them, daring her to turn her back on them.

"Do you approve, Reed?" she whispered into the air, then laughed aloud to cover the sentimentality of the moment. But she couldn't help thinking Reed *would* approve—at least in part. He would like Doug's comportment on the course and his obvious affection for Dean, and maybe even his irreverence. Reed, for all his natural dignity and innate conservatism, had certainly never been a stuffed shirt, proven by the fact that he'd batted aside, as if they were so many cobwebs, the objections raised by his sister-in-law when he'd decided to marry Laurel.

Much as she hated to wash away the traces of her loving hour with Dean, Laurel felt that a shower and shampoo were definitely in order. There was a real world out there beyond the secure white walls of her house, and since at the moment its intentions toward her weren't entirely friendly, she had to gird herself for battle. She had sympathy in her heart for Eleanor Campion Ligeret, knowing that even the most selfish of mothers would have to shed many hot tears over a child she'd left behind. But suddenly to reappear, after all the years of silence, seemingly without any regard to the impact her arrival might have on her child—did she have any justification for her act? Uneasily, Laurel reminded herself that she still had to break the news to Dean. Or should she wait until Eleanor Ligeret had actually set foot on American soil? A woman with her history was entirely capable of changing her mind and postponing the maternal visit for another decade. Toweling herself dry, Laurel decided to confer with the friends she sometimes laughingly referred to as her board of directors—Elsie and Pete Howard and Webb Daniels.

First, though, she would call Doug, and know that she had the balm of his presence coming to her at the end of what promised to be a trying day.

As she waited for the Hilton operator to connect her with Doug's room, Laurel cast affectionate glances at a bed that still showed the impress of his body, faintly redolent of his spice.

"Hello?" a woman's voice said.

"Operator?" Laurel stammered.

"Not me," the voice at the other end said cheerfully. "You want Doug, eh? And who does not?"

"Is Mr. Stewart available?" Laurel replied stiffly, automatically retreating to coolness and formality in response to the other woman's cheekiness. Judging from the lilt in her voice and that telltale "eh," Laurel assumed that she, like Doug, was from Toronto. How long and how well she had known Doug was anybody's guess, but some of the possibilities struck Laurel as distinctly unpleasant.

"Doug-las," the woman called. "It's for a Mr. Stewart. Do we have one of those around?"

"Cut it out, Clare," Laurel heard Doug say crossly, her heart soaring at the sound of his voice. "Hello?" he said into the phone.

"Hi, Doug," she said, willing the frostiness he hated to melt away. "It's Laurel."

"Darling!" he exclaimed, sounding as glad and relieved to hear her voice as though he hadn't heard it in months. "How do you feel?"

"Don't you know how she feels?" Laurel heard the other woman call out, clearly more than happy to have her voice carry through the telephone wires.

"Clare, go lock yourself in the bathroom," Doug said sharply. "Or go downstairs and buy yourself a lurid romance to read. This is private." Then he said into the telephone, "Sorry, darling. That's Clare Hamilton. She's a sports reporter from Toronto who's the bane of my existence. Are you better? You sound better?"

"After medicine like that, who wouldn't be better?" Laurel said lightly, masking over her churning emotions.

"We're on for tonight, then, eh?" Doug said. "Lobster sound good to you? I'll rent a car if you don't feel up to driving. Or maybe we should go back to the Farmingdale River Inn and gorge ourselves on mashed turnips."

"Can we work out the details later?" Laurel asked. "I love the idea of double-dating with Dean and Ginny, and they may have some ideas. They probably know the fun spots around Hartford better than I do."

"What about the sightseeing?" Doug asked. "I hear that the public can see Mark Twain's house and that it's worth the detour—and you know how interested I am in anyone who understands the New England weather!"

"It *is* a beautiful Victorian house," Laurel said, "with a great collection of Tiffany glass, but do you think maybe we could postpone seeing it? Some family business has come up, and I've been a little slow getting myself together. I think we'd better just plan on dinner."

"All right," Doug agreed, a little too quickly for Laurel's taste. "Suppose I call you around five. Ow!" he suddenly exclaimed, and Laurel heard female giggles in the backgound. "Clare," she heard him scold, "you have the sense of humor of a five-year-old! Sorry, darling," he said into the telephone. "You know how it is. Some reporters will do anything to get a story."

"Of course," Laurel trilled, feeling utterly phony but determined not to let Doug know what discomfiting turns her imagination was taking. "Bye, darling," she said, hanging up before she had to hear anything more from or about one Clare Hamilton.

The woman's name was familiar, Laurel realized, as she slipped into a lacy bra and panties and sat down at her dressing table to dry her hair. A sports reporter from Toronto . . . of course. Laurel had read a capsule profile on her in one of those women-on-the-way-up magazine articles she glanced at when she was in the dentist's waiting room, or maybe it had been at the Hair Place in West Hartford, where Lewis took a quarter inch off her hair every three weeks.

Clare Hamilton, the first woman sports reporter for one of the Toronto dailies, had gone to court to force the Canadian hockey teams to let her into their locker rooms with the male press for post-game interviews. Laurel didn't remember whether Clare had won or lost her case, but she very clearly remembered the mischievous pixie face in the postage-stamp size photograph accompanying the profile and an impression, left by the article, that Clare Hamilton knew what she wanted and didn't mind fighting for it.

Just Doug Stewart's type, Laurel thought miserably. Scrappy, irreverent, unfettered by belief in the proprieties. Had she come to Connecticut to see him play—or to play with him? Laurel looked into her dressing table mirror and saw a beautiful woman, but one who was well beyond the pixie girl stage. Wasn't that a silver thread among the gold of her hair? A new wrinkle at the corner of each eye? No doubt Doug had been genuinely attracted to her and had seen her as part of the challenge of Falling Water, but that didn't have a lot to do with a wondrous future along the lines Laurel's mind had been rapidly traveling. Only yesterday morning she'd reminded Elsie Howard that touring pros were notorious womanizers, and that Doug looked as though he fit the classic definition; yet a kiss and a soft word had blazed away any semblance of caution on her part. Angrily brushing and blowing her hair, Laurel decided that Clare Hamilton was probably the thoroughly modern sort of young woman who wore designer sweatsuits to cocktail parties and smiled tolerantly on her men friends' doings with other women. Even now, she was probably cozying up to Doug on his rented bed, toying familiarly with his body, coaxing him to spill the details of his erotic passage with Laurel.

"Damn you for a fool, Laurel Campion!" she told the mirror, then burst out laughing. In her anger she had pulled every last suggestion of wavy softness out of her hair, had disciplined it into what had to be considered a severe angularity, even by local standards. It would take a scarfless ride in her Mercedes to ruffle *that* head. She felt a little spurt of satisfaction, as though she'd somehow gotten back at Doug for being alone in a hotel room with Clare Hamilton... maybe for having been alone in many hotel rooms with Clare Hamilton.

Glancing at her clock, she realized that Dean would be home any minute. She quickly applied the minimal makeup she used by day and got into an impeccably tailored blue and white seersucker suit that allowed her to feel crisp and cool on even the most wilting of summer days, then called Webb Daniels's office.

"He's in a meeting at the governor's office, Mrs. Campion," his secretary said, "but I'll call him there if it's urgent."

Deciding that any situation involving Dean merited preferential treatment, Laurel told the secretary that the matter *was* urgent, then sat by her telephone tapping her fingernails on her bedside table until Webb called back.

"What's up, Laurel?" he asked, his voice concerned. Listening to her news about Eleanor Campion Ligeret's impending arrival, he wasted no time on commentary but simply said, "I'll meet you at my office at four o'clock."

Laurel next dialed Elsie Howard's number, but got no answer. Friday . . . three o'clock . . . the twins' swimming lessons, Laurel calculated. She was about to call Pete Howard at his office when the telephone rang, and it was Pete calling her.

"You had the phone off the hook?" he asked. "Elsie was trying you and trying you and was getting ready to come break down your doors, but I persuaded her that you were probably asleep. Feeling better?"

"Terrific—except that Dean's mother is reportedly on her way to the States to try to scoop him up."

"The hell she is!" Pete exploded. "You're kidding me."

"I'm not. I have it straight from Sara's mouth. She's due in at Bradley late Saturday afternoon. Evan and Sara are going to meet her plane."

"They are? Since when the hell are they so friendly with Eleanor? Laurel, something smells fishy here. I was Eleanor's internist, and I know the OB who delivered Dean—and I didn't argue with him for a minute when he told me that she put the lie to the notion of maternal instincts. She only had a baby because Reed pressured her into it. She never gave a damn about anyone or anything but her painting. And she wasn't so such-a-much of an artist, if you ask me."

"I've got a meeting with Webb in a little while to see if we can do anything on the legal front. But it's not really a legal issue, is it, Pete? I mean, should I try to stop Dean if he—if he wants to go back to France with her?"

There was silence at the other end, and Laurel knew Pete was filling a pipe. Though he had bullied most of his patients into giving up cigarettes, he said every human being needed a relatively harmless outlet for stress, and his was a pipe once a week or so. "Certainly they have every right to see each other," Pete said, "every moral right, and I have to guess it would be a healthy thing for Dean. He's probably turned her into a kind of myth figure in his mind, made her either a devil or a saint, and it can only help him to know she's just another mortal human being."

"He never brings her up," Laurel said, "and if someone else does, he changes the subject as quickly as he can."

"I know. I know. For all his talk about letting it hang out, that's one hand he plays very close to the chest. But I'm sure about this, Laurel. He's crazy about you. Eleanor's important to him, but you're real to him. The only thing that would drive him to her would be anything on your part he can construe as rejection. So if he gets excited about seeing her and feels a bit puffed up because she makes a fuss over him, keep your head on straight. Don't take his excitement as rejection of you and then turn around and take it out on him. Got it?"

"Yes, doctor."

"But I don't have to tell you about how to swallow your emotions! By the way," he went on cheerfully, "if I see Eleanor, I'll probably strangle her. You've been that boy's mother, and I think she has one helluva nerve drumming up some big maternal act. I wonder if Sara—" His voice trailed off, and Laurel heard the sound of meditative pipe sucking. "No. Unworthy," he said obscurely, then wished her luck and hung up.

A distinctly unladylike gurgle reminded her that she hadn't yet put solid food into her stomach that day. Laurel started down to the kitchen to make tea and cinnamon toast. Elsie's cracked wheat bread smelled wonderful in the toaster, and Laurel realized thankfully that health was hers again. Lord, she was a lucky woman, she thought, as she spread butter and honey over the hot toast, then sprinkled powered cinnamon onto the lovely, gooey surface she'd created. To have Dean, to have health, to live the good life among true friends in beautiful Farming-dale . . . did she really need more at this time in her life? So what if her amorous entanglement with Doug Stewart proved to have been an interlude, not the prelude she'd hoped it was? She wasn't some innocent kid, feeling betrayed and cheated because he belonged to Clare Hamilton. Damned if she wasn't glad she'd met him and done everything she'd done with him. Even if she was merely one more country-club conquest to him.

Just as she was starting anxiously to wonder if Dean was going to get home before she had to leave for Webb's office, he came zooming up the driveway, his fine old wood-paneled station wagon rattling as he arrived.

"Hey, you're all better," he exclaimed. "Where you going?"

"I just suddenly got a shopping bug," she said, none too happy to be lying but not wanting to tell Dean the big news when she had only five minutes to talk to him. "Mr. Stewart—Doug—wants to know if you and Ginny would like to double-date with us for dinner. We were thinking about driving to Niantic for lobster, unless you have some better idea."

"Wow! Can I have a drink tonight? A beer, anyway?"

"Absolutely not," Laurel said firmly. She let him have a beer at home if he wasn't going to be driving, but in public she insisted that he stick to the law, even in restaurants that were less than thorough about checking IDs.

"I'll be eighteen next month," Dean said defiantly.

"I'm well aware," Laurel said, turning away to conceal the sadness she was afraid she'd let slip to the surface. She was sure that Eleanor Ligeret had a much more relaxed attitude than she about matters like alcohol—especially if she'd married a man who came from the great wine-producing region of Burgundy. Would she draw Dean away with promises of a worldly, faintly decadent existence?

As she drove along Route 84 into downtown Hartford, Laurel wondered if she'd been too strict with Dean, too conservative, over-mothering him to make up for his absence of real parents. Maybe instead of lecturing him about becoming motivated, she should have taken him traveling more, letting him discover all the enticements of the world. They'd gone skiing a couple of times during the winter, and she'd taken him to Boca Raton for a golfing vacation during his February intercession, but skiing and golf had been part of his life since early boyhood, and the people he met at Stowe and Boca were pretty much of a piece with the people he'd always known. Loomis, the private school he attended, was relatively progressive and liberal for a prep school and had students from many backgrounds, but it hadn't yet electrified his mind or been an eye-opener for him. Laurel wondered if maybe she shouldn't hope for Dean's sake that Eleanor would offer him the excitement of a European education. Well, maybe she *should* hope for it, but she didn't, and she wasn't going to pretend to. She could take him to Europe herself. She *would* take him to Europe herself. Or not herself. If she and Doug—

She forced her mind away from that dangerous "if." She hadn't canceled her dinner date with Doug, despite the disturbing presence of another woman in his hotel room, because she wanted Dean and Ginny to have their glamorous evening with a man who showed every possibility of becoming a mid-life athletic superstar. And, *be honest, Laurel!*, she hadn't canceled it because she couldn't help hoping that she'd misguessed the relationship between Doug and Clare Hamilton, though she wouldn't want to bank on it. Doug was probably a sometime thing—and Dean was forever; and she herself, famous take-charge lady that she was, would take Dean to Europe. If he chose to stay with her.

"Of course he'll want to stay with you," Webb boomed loyally, as she leaned back against the thick, wine-color leather cushions of the armchair that faced his desk. Webb's office was on the top floor of one of the buildings in the complex called Constitution Plaza, and his generous windows offered views of the Connecticut River and some of the more decorative modern office buildings of downtown Hartford—the glinting Gold Building, with a metallic facade the color of its name, and the deep turquoise glass ovoid that housed the Phoenix Mutual Life Insurance Company. If she craned her neck, Laurel knew she could see the stately, older spires of the Nutmeg State Life Insurance Company, where Reed had once been president and she had once been a secretary; but she didn't want to crane her neck. This was a day to look to the future, not the past.

"Are you so sure, Webb?" she asked. "Eleanor is bound to fascinate him, and who knows what exotic offers she'll make. Summers on the Mediterranean, skiing in the Alps, the museums of Paris—"

Waving his hand dismissively, Webb said, "Nonsense, old girl. Dean may talk a lot about saving the world, but he's never said much about seeing the world. I think he'd just as soon stick to good old Farmingdale. But we can't take any chances, can we?" He gave a meaningful tap to the white telephone sitting to the left of his immaculate leatherbound blotter.

"What do you mean?" Laurel asked.

"I've got connections in the Immigration Department. I could arrange to block Eleanor's entry into the country."

"But how?" Laurel stammered, "She's an American citizen."

"Not any more, she isn't. She gave up her citizenship when she married this Ligeret. Apparently his family set great store by her becoming a French citizen, and she set great store by his family's money—and the rest is history. She always was a great one for renouncing one thing and taking up another."

Letting the information sink in, Laurel asked, "How do you know all this, Webb?"

"I took the liberty of telephoning Sara. I figured time was of the essence here."

"And Eleanor gave Sara all that information in one transatlantic call? I'm glad I'm not paying the phone bill!"

Webb looked uncomfortable. "Actually, old girl, Sara and Eleanor have been in touch for some time."

"I see," Laurel said. She didn't see, in fact, but she knew that Webb's friendship with Evan and Sara Campion went back twenty years, and she didn't want him to feel split between his loyalty to them and his loyalty to her. When he didn't volunteer any further information, she got up and walked to the window, staring at the quiet flow of the river and at the timeless view of East Hartford on the far bank.

"Laurel," Webb began, "I know that Sara hasn't always been exactly sisterly toward you, but you have to understand how your arrival in Farmingdale undid her life plan."

"Oh, I'm sure," Laurel mumured. "No doubt she had some proper young blueblood picked out to succeed Eleanor."

"I have to concede that Sara isn't the most democratic spirit ever to exist," Webb said. "But her unhappiness had to do with a lot more than your lack of Pilgrim ancestors. She's always taken it very hard that she and Evan couldn't have children, and I think she had cast herself in the long run role of Dean's surrogate mother."

"Sara?" Laurel asked, surprised and confused. "But she's always complaining about little kids making too much noise in the grillroom, and teenage girls not covering up their bikinis in the snack bar at the pool—" She paused as her eye caught sight of a small barge making its way down the river. Something about the craft's inelegant motions made her smile. "Do people ever barge down the river for fun?" she asked, dreamily. "I wonder if Dean would like to do that. Probably a lot more adventure than going for a polite sail out of Fisher's Island." And what about rafting the white water of the Colorado River? She could so easily picture Doug and Dean and herself, shrieking with ecstasy and fear as they rocked and rolled through the rapids and felt the sting of the spray hard against their faces—

And if she didn't pay attention to what Webb was saying, she might lose Dean as well as Doug. By heaven, what with one thing and another, she was getting to be a real pro at losing her beloved men.

Sauntering over to the window, Webb put a friendly arm around Laurel's shoulders. "I know this business with Eleanor is hard on you, but don't make Sara the scapegoat. Don't you see that all her impatience with other people's feelings is just a reflection of the emptiness she feels? That big house of theirs, with all those unlived-in rooms—"

"And that's why she's conspiring to have Eleanor take Dean away from me? So we can have un-lived-in rooms in our big house? She *is* conspiring with her, isn't she, Webb?" She looked hard at her old friend and thought she saw beads of perspiration on his forehead, though the office was comfortably air-conditioned. "This business about the Immigration Department was just a distraction, wasn't it? You know I would never use means like that to keep Eleanor from getting to Dean. Imagine his resentment toward me if he ever found out—and these things always do get found out. Anyway, it's wrong, and I won't go for it, and I want to know just whose side you're on. There's some other twist here, isn't there?"

"God, you're beautiful today," Webb said, his voice thickening. "In a way I think you're even more beautiful in that suit and with your hair that way than you were last night. May I kiss you?"

Moving a step backward, Laurel said, "Your sense of timing is appalling, Webb. I'm astonished. I didn't know *we* behaved this way," she added, mimicking Sara's haughty tones. For all his self-proclaimed rudeness and crudeness, Doug Stewart would never have made a move toward her when her heart and mind were brimming with fears about losing Dean. A comforting kiss, a gentle stroking of her hair, maybe, but not a pass.

"Laurel, Laurel—"

"Don't 'Laurel, Laurel' me," she said coolly.

Webb stood so perfectly still for a long moment that he reminded Laurel of the mannequins in the windows at Henry Miller's, the Civic Center shop that clothed the most demanding of the Hartford area men. Bowing his gray head a fraction, he said, "I apologize. I've held so much in for so long, and last night you seemed to be inviting me to open the floodgates—only you weren't, were you?"

Mutely Laurel shook her head.

"What is it about him, Laurel?" Webb asked. "Of course he's younger than I am—"

"Who is younger than you are, Webb?" She knew perfectly well, but in her anger she wanted to force Webb to say the name.

"That Doug Stewart. How can you? I thought you were a true Farmingdale Campion. He—" Words seemed to catch in his throat.

"He what?" Laurel rapped out.

"Those jeans of his!" Webb exclaimed. "Never before in all my life have I seen a professional golfer wear faded blue jeans in a major PGA event. It's disgraceful."

Bursting into great peals of laughter, Laurel could only gasp, "Webb, oh, Webb. That's the funniest thing I ever heard." She wiped her eyes with the back of her hand. "Dean wears faded jeans on the course. And if he isn't a Farmingdale Campion, who is?"

"He's a child. It's a phase he's going through. Adolescent rebellion. For a grown man, and a pro, dress is a different matter."

"You think so, counselor? Well, I'm glad I know what your priorities are now. Thanks for the advice." Swinging her white leather shoulder bag with jaunty abandon, she marched out of his office.

chapter

8

REALIZING THAT SHE would never make it back to Farmingdale in time to receive Doug's promised five o'clock call, Laurel decided to call him from one of the pay phones in the lobby of Webb's building. The lilt of his deep voice was like a summons to exotic ports, and Laurel had all she could do to convey simple information. Some unruly spirit within her, the author of all those wild fantasies of hers, longed to throw caution to the wind and send her hurtling into his strong arms.

"Look," Doug was saying, "why drive all the way back to Farmingdale now? We can meet at some local spot for an un-drink, eh? Then Dean and his girl can join us at whatever restaurant we pick. What do you think about a Japanese meal instead of lobster? Clare's been in Hartford before, and she says there's a good one, complete with tatami room, at the Civic Center."

Gritting her teeth at the sound of Clare's name, Laurel prattled, "Dean will be thrilled at the idea of the tatami room. He's convinced that eating cross-legged is better for the digestion. But there's a family matter I have to discuss with him, and—well, I'm dressed very much à la Lady Blue, and I was hoping to try to pass for Laurie tonight."

"Well, go buy some Laurie rags, and change in my hotel room. I'll be glad to help you undress," he teased, forcing Laurel to conjure the not totally unpleasant memory of his flagrantly sensual eye work when she'd stood naked before him. "And can't the business with Dean hold until after dinner? From the tone of your voice, it's not the sort of family business that's going to improve anyone's digestion—so why ruin his evening by feeding him an unpleasant appetizer?"

"Better to feed him an unpleasant dessert, you mean!" But Laurel had to agree Doug had a point. A realistic inner voice reminded her that the Doug Stewart fantasy was probably going to be over in a day or so for Dean as well as herself, and it did seem rather a shame to fill his head full of Eleanor before the big double date. Who could tell how Dean would take the news of her impending visit and her intentions? He might be so overcome, so torn, that he'd retreat to his messy room and his music and refuse to go to dinner at all.

"All right," Laurel agreed. "I'll call Dean from here, then go find myself a dress. That will make an honest woman of me, anyway. I told Dean I was coming to town to shop." Thinking what a relief it was going to be to snuggle up to Doug later and tell him about all the goings-on of the day, she suddenly caught herself up short. *When* was she going to snuggle up to Doug? Suddenly he'd rewritten the scenario for the evening so she had a late date with her stepson! Was it because *he* had a late date with a pixie-faced reporter from Toronto?

As if reading the name looming large in her mind, Doug said, "By the way, mind if Clare Hamilton joins us for drinks? She's dying to meet you. She's working on a big article about American women golfers."

"Yes, I want to know if it's true that they hold the club differently from the way Canadian women do," a loud voice called from the background, a giggling undertone making it altogether apparent that Laurel was entirely welcome to interpret the double meaning of the remark.

How like Doug she was, Laurel thought, a wave of misery sweeping over her. No doubt the two of them would have a lot of laughs as soon as Lady Prim hung up the phone. Not much she could do about the laughs, but she could deny them the satisfaction of knowing that they'd cut her to the quick. Were they in bed at this very minute, or were they putting off that particular pleasure until after dinner? "Terrific!" Laurel enthused. "I'm dying to meet her." Then, rashly, not knowing she was going to utter the words until they were out of her mouth, she said, "Suppose I ask Webb Daniels to join us if he's free. He's got a lot of curiosity about you."

"Has he just!" Doug thundered. "What did I tell you about the effects of jealousy?" Laughing softly, he added, "Why not? Some party, eh?" Apparently happy enough to forget he'd invited her to change her clothes in his hotel room, Doug suggested that she and Webb meet him and Clare in the Hilton lobby at six. "Then you and I can meet Dean and Ginny at the Tokyo Garden at seven-thirty. You won't mind being seen alone on the streets of Hartford with me for the stroll to the restaurant, will you?"

Her heart sinking at the return of his old, jibing turn of phrase, Laurel returned bitingly, "At least you've set up things so I don't have to be seen alone with you strolling *away* from the restaurant."

She called Dean to let him know the arrangements,

then started back across the giant black and white check-
erboard squares of the lobby to the bank of elevators. If
golf was a metaphor for life, as she'd told Dean during
the pro-am event the day before, then she'd sure enough
hit her way square into the bunker with her notion about
bringing Webb to meet Doug and Clare for drinks. Then
again, if her game had a particular strength, it was her
ability to hit her way out of sand and other awkward lies
of the ball.

"Webb," she said, as his secretary showed her into
his office for the second time that day, "I want to apologize. I overreacted before. I'm rather a mama tiger when
it comes to Dean, you know. You've been a good friend,
and I—"

"I'm the one who should apologize," Webb interrupted, holding out his hands. "I've been tearing my hair
ever since you left, waiting for you to get home so I
could call you. I let two very important issues get mixed
up, and that was stupid and reprehensible of me. Like
Sara and Evan, I guess I've always seen Dean as the
closest thing I would ever have to a son, and when it
became so damned obvious that this Doug Stewart and
you were getting along famously, I panicked. I imagined
losing you and Dean all at once. When you called me
and told me about Eleanor's latest scheme, I imagined
being your tower of strength . . . and, well, I guess Sara
and I both thought that if you and I got together, Dean
wouldn't possibly want to go away. You've been a real
mother to him, old girl, don't misunderstand, but a boy
does need a father, too, and he and I have always had
a very cordial relationship. Besides, Dean is a real home-
town boy."

For the second time that day, Laurel found herself
thinking about cigarettes and half wishing she hadn't
quit. Then again, she'd quit precisely because Laurel
Campion wasn't supposed to need crutches! "You mean,"
she said to Webb, "you thought I was going to just go

off with Doug and forget about Dean, or else drag him along to some new environment without giving him any say in the matter? Given which situation, he'd embrace Eleanor in one damn big hurry?"

Running his fingers through his gray hair, Webb said unhappily that he and Sara had harbored such unworthy thoughts.

"Well, Sara must have loved the part about me leaving town," Laurel said grimly, though she'd vowed in the elevator that this was going to be a conciliatory meeting.

"No, no, not at all," Webb insisted, "Sara doesn't dislike you, Laurel. She's just deeply jealous of your relationship with Dean, can't you see? And, of course, you're young and beautiful—" He turned away and coughed a social cough—perhaps fearing, Laurel thought, that he'd once again made a move out of line. Poor dear Webb! And poor Sara and Evan with their barren house! A thought came to Laurel's mind, and she ticketed it for priority handling as soon as matters at home were taken care of.

"If I may ask," Webb said, "what are your feelings about Doug Stewart? I realize that it's none of my—"

"Oh, I don't mind telling you." Her voice cool and steady, she said, "I love him, Webb, and I'm going to marry him. He and Dean and I are going to live here and there and everywhere, and be a happy family forever after. Want to join us for drinks? But you mustn't say a word. He doesn't know yet, you see."

Upsetting Laurel's preconceived notions, Clare Hamilton turned out to be an effervescent young woman who was impossible not to like. Even Webb Daniels, the existence of whose funnybone Laurel had sometimes doubted, was quickly belly laughing at her anecdotes about her adventures as a lone woman reporter in the raunchy world of male athletics. With a sisterly wink at Laurel, Clare drew Webb into a discussion about the conjunction of sports, law, and the press, leaving Doug and Laurel virtually on their own in the pleasantly dark, walnut-paneled bar on Ann Street where they'd gone for drinks.

The nearness of Doug on the leather banquette next to her brought their afternoon idyll back to her with a heady rush, and the scent of his spice in her nostrils made her feel absolutely giddy. Her body sang; her mind was in an uproar. No sooner did her consciousness acknowledge his incredible physical sway over her than a thousand warning bells went off, and no sooner did the bells go off than a thousand hands reached to stay them. Doug Stewart was a fantasy, one voice said; Doug Stewart was the ultimate reality, another voice said. Doug Stewart was someone to delight in for the very brief present . . . Doug Stewart was her man for all seasons. Had she really told Webb she was going to marry this man? Yes, and she would—if she didn't turn her back on him forever that evening.

A ray of light played across his face, and she had to bite her tongue to keep from crying out her desire for him. He wasn't handsome, but he was beautiful, the eyes relentlessly questing, the weathery seams of his face making a striking contrast with the oddly patrician lines of his nose. Reed's had been an accessible face, an even-featured, smooth, serene visage she had memorized easily after the first glance. Doug's face was somehow elusive. She felt that, like his temper, it could change without warning, that just when she thought she had it by heart, it would surprise her. That faint dimple to the left of his mouth—had it been there a minute ago? And a minute later it might turn into the one-sided sneer he was apt to produce on any excuse.

"You must be impossible to photograph," she murmured. "A movie camera, yes, but how does a still camera get it all?"

"I've been accused of being twins," Doug laughed. "Fraternal twins."

Bridling at the idea that another woman—it had to be a woman—had thought what she was thinking, had felt what she was feeling, Laurel did her best to cover her emotions by asking, "Do you have a brother, in fact?"

"Several of them," Doug rasped.

"And your parents?" she asked hesitantly, knowing how little he liked personal questions, how quick he was to interpret them as a reflection of snobbish anxieties on her part.

"I'm a poor little orphan, like you," he returned, in one of those voices she couldn't quite fathom—except that it clearly contained a warning that she was trespassing on forbidden territory.

From across the table, pixie-faced Clare hooted. "Not your poor little orphan routine, Douglas! Now that—"

"Shush up," he ordered. "Anyone over there need a drink freshened up?"

"This is my round, Doug," Webb said amiably, as though they'd been bar buddies forever.

"Thanks," Doug said, "but one Shirley Temple's my limit. How about you, Laurel?"

Not daring to drink alcohol on her nearly empty stomach, Laurel had ordered mineral water. She gestured at her brimming glass. "I'm fine, thanks, gentlemen," she said.

"Well, someone's got to keep the north-of-the-border liquor industry going," Clare announced merrily. "I'll have another Canadian and ginger."

"And I'm ready for another Scotch," Webb chimed in.

The jukebox was playing the vintage jazz Laurel liked so much, and the smoky, talky cluster of humanity contributed to her very pleasant feeling of being off duty, but when Doug said he wanted to get a breath of fresh air and stretch his legs, she didn't hesitate for a second about joining him.

As they made their way through the crowd, a young woman in a pink linen suit took a look at Doug, gasped, and reached out to grab his arm. "Aren't you Doug Stewart?" she trilled. "You were just terrific today. We were allowed to have the TV on at the office all day because my boss is a golf buff."

"Well, you've got Doug Stewart in the flesh, Cindy!" someone in her crowd declared.

"Oh, no she doesn't," Doug replied with a smile. "The flesh is reserved for the lady in seersucker."

"Knock 'em dead tomorrow, Doug," a mustached young bartender called out as they neared the door.

"Well, rabbit," Laurel said, taking his arm as they got to the sidewalk, "you're not exactly an unknown anymore. You've really got some fans."

"They would have warmed to anyone they recognized from TV who walked in there," Doug said. "Me or Tom Watson or some actor who plays a heart surgeon on one of the soaps. It wasn't exactly personal, eh?"

"No, I disagree," Laurel said. "I thought it was very personal. Everyone gets excited at the idea of a newcomer to the field outplaying the old-timers. Especially one who's—"

"Who's what?"

"Well, you're not exactly a kid. Most rabbits are— you know—in their early twenties, and they have all that raw strength to whack the ball with. Look, that's the railroad station. Isn't it spooky? They've been talking about renovating it for twenty years."

"Decrepit," Doug commented, "just like me." He pulled her back from the curb as a taxi squealed around the corner from Union Place.

"I didn't mean you were decrepit, and you know it, Doug Stewart! But why..." Taking a deep breath, she plunged boldly into the line of questioning that was always so risky. "Why did you join the tour at this stage of the game? Obviously you didn't become a great golfer overnight!"

"Hardly!" he agreed, sounding amused. "I was born a golfer like little John Coover. I should have joined the tour when I was younger but I didn't have the sense to. But that doesn't mean I won't know when to quit the tour." His grin faded. "Nothing more pathetic, is there, than a touring pro who doesn't know when to retire? Placing sixty-third in a field of sixty-four? And all the nights in hotel rooms, and the meals in restaurants, and the plane rides in bad weather when you wonder what you're up there for—"

"Then what do you see as your future?" Laurel bravely probed.

"The carousel."

"The what?"

"I want to ride the carousel in Bushnell Park with you in the very immediate future. Isn't it just a block over this way? Sure, I can see the Hilton."

They started toward the park in silence. Union Place, the long block bounded on one side by the old railroad station and on the other by boutiques, was Hartford's miniature equivalent of Greenwich Village, and as they passed an antique dress shop, Laurel felt it catch Doug's attention. "I know," she said. "That's the sort of thing you'd like me to wear, isn't it? That peach-colored chemise that looks to me as though it should have another dress to cover it up? Or that red one? I'd swear it's nothing but a big scarf."

"Yes, what happened to your shopping spree, *Laurie?* You look very much like Mrs. Laurel Campion dressed to meet her lawyer. Not that you're not beautiful—" Swinging her around into his arms, he said, "You could wear seersucker by day and burlap by night and I'd still be wild about you. You know that, don't you? I'm not in the business of changing people—least of all the most enticing woman I've ever met. If you have to be untrue to yourself to be true to me, it's no good, eh?" Letting his lips meet hers in a soft, restrained kiss, he released her.

"What you mean, don't you, is that I'm a more interesting challenge in seersucker?" Laurel returned bitingly. "Playing me is like playing the fifth hole at Falling Water, with those dense stands of maple in the rough and those tricky bunkers and a green that outsmarts the best of them. If you..."

"Now, wait a minute, Lady Blue. I don't mind doing battle with you when there's a legitimate dispute between us, but I refuse to let you—I absolutely forbid you—to twist my words around that way. That's so unfair it's like..." His lips curling, he went on, "It's like improving your lie when you're supposed to be playing by summer rules. Now maybe that's acceptable to the country club set—"

"Oh, so you forbid me, do you?" Laurel echoed angrily, drawing her spine an impossible fraction taller and straighter.

A train whistle sounded, as the 6:09 to Springfield crossed the bridge over Bushnell Park and rolled toward the station, fifteen minutes late as usual. For no reason that Laurel could fathom, the sound of the whistle and the sight of the two-car train provoked bubbling laughter in her and Doug, clearing the air between them.

"The good Lord help us if we ever try to discuss anything genuinely controversial," Doug said, as their laughter subsided. "Politics, criminal justice, child-rearing. How should we raise our kids, do you think?" he added lightly.

Hoping that the pounding of her heart wasn't audible, Laurel answered in a tone meant to match his, "Lots and lots of love, and they have to learn at an early age to keep their eyes on the ball and the left wrist firm."

"And never play by winter rules?"

"Never," Laurel agreed. The fantasy of having children with Doug suddenly too exquisite to bear, she said, "Look, I really do want to go into that shop and buy a dress. I can't ride on a carousel in a suit."

His hazel eyes clouding over, Doug said shortly, "All right." As soon as they were inside the little shop he threw himself into the search for the perfect Laurie dress, but Laurel couldn't get away from the notion that she'd managed, once again, to displease him. So she'd been right, after all: he, too, went for the ice maiden act. Yet in bed he had wanted no reticence from her, no pretended reluctance. He had been as aroused by her teeth on his earlobes as by the arched throat she'd submissively offered to his teeth. Well, Laurie was a real part of herself and, damn him, he was going to have to accept that part if he wanted her.

"How about this little number, eh?" Doug suggested, pulling something nile green and nightgownish off the rack.

"That's super on," the proprietess of the shop commented. Her own taste ran to a wild mop of champagne-color curls and layer upon layer of clothes in differently patterned fabrics—a flower print skirt that came almost to her ankles, a long purple shirt with billowing sleeves, a vest in a different flower print. Laurel wasn't sanguine that their definitions of "super" coincided. "It's from the forties," the other woman went on. "The real thing. I picked it up in Soho last time I was in New York. If you like it, I'll knock ten bucks off the sticker price. To tell you the truth, it looks lousy unless you can wear it without a bra, and most of the women around here are either too big up top or else uptight about going braless."

Doug raised his thick Scots eyebrow. Laurel was sure that he didn't for a moment think she'd so much as try on the dress—that both he and the shop owner were taunting her. A lot they knew about her!

"It's just what I've been looking for," she gushed.

Pointing to the doorway partially covered by an Indian-print bedspread tacked to the top of the frame, she asked, "Is that the dressing room?"

"Uh-huh," the other woman said. "You can both go in. I don't expect any other customers," she added dismally, stooping to neaten a display of old scarves, worn but carefully ironed, in a display case.

Blond head high, Laurel preceded Doug through the doorway. The dressing room was also a storage room, with boxes piled everywhere and a single light bulb for illumination, but if Doug thought she was going to screech or faint or make some snide comment, he had another guess coming. Taking off her suit jacket and tossing it over a carton, she began to unbutton the white silk shirt she wore underneath.

"May I be of service, madame?" Doug inquired, hanging the green dress from a hook.

"Please," she said haughtily. "It's so tiresome to unbutton one's own buttons."

"I understand madame's point perfectly." Avoiding her eyes, letting no smile intrude on the mood of the little fantasy, Doug undid her buttons with a body servant's impersonal deftness.

Slipping off the shirt and handing it to him, Laurel said, "Kindly unfasten my brassiere. I do dislike having to reach behind my own back."

"But madame should never have to reach behind her own back. Such a beautiful back," he murmured, in a decidedly unservile voice, his fingers tracing her shoulder blades, then tiptoeing down to the waistband of her skirt, and beneath it.

Standing with her breasts exposed in the communal dressing room, only a thin piece of cloth separating her and Doug from the proprietess and anyone else who might wander into the shop, Laurel felt her creamy, swelling skin tingle and flame in response to a sensation she couldn't name. Then, as Doug slowly turned her around and pulled her to him, she realized what the sensation was. *She was very nearly out of control.* She was a character in someone else's fantasy, and it was a sublime thing to be because the someone else was Doug and she loved him and he was repeating her name over and over again with a sweet intensity that made her want to let go completely.

"How's it look? You need any help with that zipper?" the shop owner called in.

"We're doing fine," Laurel called back, the steadiness of her voice astonishing her—though wasn't steadiness her calling card? The woman who never whiffed in the rough, who hardly ever three-putted a green, even in the heat of competition? Sure, even when she'd been Laurie, wearing a big smile to go with her frilly blouse, joking around with the regular customers at the Farmingdale River Inn as she served them their drinks, she'd been calm and reliable and very much a take-charge woman.

"We are doing fine, aren't we?" Doug whispered tenderly, brushing a strand of hair back from her cheek, then kissing the cheek, kissing her eyes.

"Doug, I want to let go," she said. "I want to lose control—be absolutely swept out to sea—and I don't know if I can act outside of my fantasy."

"Because you think I want you to let go?" he asked gruffly.

"Because I want to feel all the feelings there are— the way you do."

"Oh, darling," he groaned, pressing her head against his chest, letting her feel his height and strength. "Do I dare believe you? I want to, but I'm not sure I dare to."

A little stiffly, covering up the hurt she felt, Laurel said, "I better try on that dress, or our friend out there is going to call the vice squad."

Stepping out of her skirt and standing in front of the mirror, Laurel saw Doug looking impassively at her reflected image, nude but for the skin-tone pantyhose she wore with her high-heeled white leather sandals. Only hours ago he'd said he longed to make love with her in front of a mirror, yet he seemed damnably well able to keep his distance from her now. Would she ever understand the workings of his mind—and would he ever understand the workings of hers? Lord, what a wearying, perilous business it was, getting to know another human being, especially when you were both well past the age of dewy innocence and rose-colored illusions.

To her amazement, the nile green dress fit her as if it had been tailored to her measurements. Though it was very different from anything in her closet, she had to concede that it had an offbeat kind of elegance to it. The draped bodice wasn't as revealing as she'd feared it would be. It suggested the outline of her breasts but was opaque enough to screen her nipples from public scrutiny. And the double strand of pearls she'd chosen to go with her suit happened to be a perfect accessory to the dress! She would have preferred a forest-green sandal to complete the look, but no one could say the white sandals she was wearing were wrong for the dress.

"I'll take it," she told the blonde in the print layers, as she emerged from the dressing room.

"What did I tell you?" the other woman said. "Super. You could wear it right out of here."

"I intend to," Laurel said, with a little smile. "If you'll just remove the tag for me." Opening her wallet and taking out a credit card, she stopped at a look on the shop owner's face. "Oh, no. You don't take credit cards? I came out without my checkbook, and I never carry large amounts of cash."

"Sorry, but with my volume of business, I can't afford to lose seven percent of my take to the card companies."

"Will you bill me, then? My name is . . ."

"No problem, darling," Doug said, coming up behind her. "I'm sure I can pay with traveler's checks, eh?"

"Right," the proprietess said. "I'll just need some ID."

"Passport do?"

"Fine. You're Canadian, aren't you?"

"Yes," Doug said. As he looked at the hastily scribbled bill and began to countersign traveler's checks, Laurel got the distinct impression that he was blocking her view of the checks with his left hand, as if there were something about them he didn't want Laurel to see. But what? Some strange middle name he was sensitive about?

"May I see your passport photo?" she asked, when the shop owner had inspected his signature and was passing the black-covered document back across the the counter.

"It's a terrible photo," he said, hastily retrieving the passport before Laurel could get ahold of it. As he stuffed the passport back into his pocket, she once again had the impression that there was something Doug Stewart was trying to hide.

chapter

9

AS THEY STOOD in line, hands clasped, for a turn on the popular, hand-painted, antique carousel, Doug and Laurel attracted a small flurry of attention from other early-evening visitors to the park. At first Laurel twitted Doug about his new recognition factor, but people weren't calling out his name, and she realized the two of them were garnering smiles and approving looks for no reason other than that they made a charming couple. Her initial self-consciousness receding about wearing so costumy a dress, she had to admit in the privacy of her mind that she and Doug were a just about perfect combination of complementary and contrasting characteristics. Both of them were tall, both of them were fair-haired, both of them exuded health and fitness. His off-white, raw silk, summer sport coat and the dark-green ascot at the open throat of his pale-green shirt echoed the eccentric chic of her dress. His ruggedness and her delicate-featured slimness were the all-important contrasting notes—a vivid declaration, Laurel thought, of their different genders.

Mostly, she realized, they looked like lovers. That was why people were smiling. What grown-ups but lovers, and new lovers at that, came to Bushnell Park in elegant garb, and stood holding hands, shivering deliciously at the relentless sounds of the calliope music?

"Want to sit in the sissy seat?" Doug teased, as the carousel wound down and unloaded.

"You can," Laurel retorted, "but I'm riding that proud beauty right there." She pointed to a white horse, its head high, its mouth open in a permanent whinny, its brown mane so realistically painted that Laurel's hand itched to stroke it.

Mounting the dark horse nearest hers, Doug said, "I hope there's no symbolism at work here! My horse is going through eternity half a length behind yours."

"But it towers over mine," Laurel pointed out, "so I guess you could say we're even."

As the carousel worked up speed, Laurel leaned over through space to share a rapturous kiss with the man on the dark horse. Dizzy, afraid of falling, she didn't know whether to blame the carousel or Doug's lips for her loss of equilibrium nor whether it was the fall of the body or the fall of the heart that she feared.

Wanted . . . feared. Wanted . . . feared. Lord, when would there be resolution? Her emotions lurching anew, she realized that all too soon this deliciously torturous limbo would come to an end. In two days the Classic would be over, the men on the tour moving on. She would know then whether she and Doug were parting forever, or whether they had a shared destiny. What should she really hope for? What did she really hope for?

When she and Doug got back to the Lady Ann bar,

they found Clare Hamilton and Webb Daniels still talking full tilt, fresh drinks in front of them.

"Did you two go out for a quick nine holes?" Clare queried sardonically, but Laurel could see she'd neither minded their absence nor resented having to spend time one-on-one with Webb. Whatever Clare and Doug were to each other or had been to each other, Clare seemed only tickled by his relationship with Laurel. Was it because was secure about her own hold on Doug and therefore didn't care if he larked about now and then? Or because they were merely friends; or because they were something in between? The last was probably the most realistic thought, Laurel concluded, not quite happily.

"I want to interview you," Clare told Laurel, "but I'm a bit sloshed."

"She likes to shock people," Webb whispered into Laurel's ear, "but actually she's very conservative underneath. I think at heart she may be more conservative than you, Laurel."

"And I bet you'd like to interview me," Clare continued. "Did you ever meet a man more close-mouthed than Doug? He only opens up when he's kissing."

"What a wit," Doug said sarcastically. He stood up. "We'd better be going, Laurel. Don't want to keep Dean and Ginny waiting."

"Dean isn't exactly famous for being on time this summer," Webb commented. "The number of times he kept me waiting at the tee—"

"I think he'll be on time tonight," Laurel said. Seeing a hurt look cross Webb's face, she added hastily, "What with Ginny being along, and all."

Webb mumbled something Laurel couldn't quite catch, and she asked him to repeat it.

"I said, I've invited Clare to dine with me at the club this evening." He gave Laurel a beseeching little look, as if to ask for her blessing.

"Oh, have you?" Laurel said. "That's nice. Don't

order the scampi, Clare. They look gorgeous, but they're tasteless."

"Just like my jokes," Clare exclaimed, breaking up.

"If you two decide to hit off a bucket, you're welcome to use my clubs. We're about the same height." The practice range was lit at night for those hard-core golf addicts who couldn't go twelve hours without the heft of a club in their hands. Several times that summer, she and Webb had doffed their dining-and-dancing garb in their respective locker rooms and made their cleated way down to the tee. "You're welcome to use anything in my locker, as far as that goes," Laurel added.

"That's very generous," Clare answered. "You're certainly welcome to anything of mine. Come to think of it, you've already helped yourself to everything of mine that counts, eh?"

Smiling as though Clare had said something amusing, Laurel led the way out of the bar. But either her mask of civility was less opaque than she'd hoped, or Doug was again able to penetrate the protective covering and see through to the truth.

"Clare and I are friends," he said, as soon as he and Laurel got to the sidewalk. "She loves to pretend she's one of the boys and make those suggestive cracks of hers, but we're friends. Not lovers. Got that?"

"It's not really my business, is it?" Laurel murmured.

"Isn't it just?" Doug thundered. "You mean all my suspicions were right? I'm just a little bit of midsummer madness for you? A way of tormenting the upright folk of Falling Water?" Turning and taking her by both shoulders, he began, "I have half a mind to—" He gave her shoulders a little shake, then turned away, a disgusted look on his face—whether aimed at her or himself, Laurel couldn't tell.

"Half a mind to what?" Laurel taunted. "Nothing too violent, I hope. Wouldn't be good publicity for the hot rabbit to be seen slugging a defenseless woman on the streets of downtown Hartford."

"Defenseless my eye," Doug muttered. "Lady, you've got more armor and offensive weapons than NATO!" His voice gentled. "Admit you were feeling jealous back there because you thought Clare and I were lovers. Come on, Lady Blue, admit that you're part of the human race, that you've got the same stock of emotions, good and bad, as the rest of us. If you meant it about wanting to let go, you're going to have to make a lot more tougher admissions, so you might as well start here."

Taking a deep breath, Laurel looked away toward the gold-coated dome of the state capitol on its bright-green rise overlooking Bushnell Park, then looked straight into Doug's eyes. She said, "I was so jealous, I thought I would turn the color of this dress. I could cheerfully have scratched her eyes, pulled her hair, and bitten off her nose. Will that do?"

Putting his hands in her hair, bending to kiss her, Doug said, "I'd call it a promising beginning."

Buoyed by the evening with Doug and Laurel and Ginny, Dean looked at the news about his mother's arrival on Saturday in what Laurel considered to be the best possible light. He was excited at the thought of seeing her, yet cushioned for the possibility of a letdown—even of a last-minute cancellation of her trip. He was inclined to be charitable about her defection. He could afford to be, he said, since he had Laurel. But he was none too eager to be vulnerable to her whim again.

"Look," he said, in his blunt, teenage way, "if she could go off and leave a helpless year-old baby, I guess she wouldn't have too much trouble deciding to leave an eighteen-year-old." Then his face got a funny expression on it, and he said, "Gee, do you think we look alike? Would we be able to pick each other out in a crowd, do you think? Am I going to feel this enormous tug in my gut when I see her and start sucking my thumb or something? Maybe I should go meet her plane with Aunt Sara and Uncle Ev. Nah—I'll let her come to me."

On one point, he was unwavering. He was glad he was going to see Eleanor, he would like maybe to take a vacation with her and get to know her. But he wasn't going to make his home with her, and not just because he was afraid to count on her. "You're my family, Laurel," he said, "and this is my home, and, well, Dad would want me to be here with you, I know. Anyway, it's where I want to be."

Assuring him again and again of her love and her wish to have him remain with her, Laurel also cautioned him not to make up his mind in advance and not to make it up too quickly in any event.

"I know, Laurel, but gee, if you'd had some child out of wedlock when you were eighteen—"

"Dean!"

"—I know you didn't do any such thing, but if you had, and it had been adopted, and now it came and said it was yours, would you kick me out to make room for it just because it was your flesh and blood?"

"I wouldn't ever kick you out to make room for anyone," Laurel said pointedly, "but—not that this ridiculous scenario of yours merits discussion—but if this child did show up, I'd want to know it, I'd want to figure out what my responsibilities toward it were, and I guess I'd try to learn to love it—maybe I would love it on first sight. You know, you can love your mother and me both. It's not a form of adultery, for heaven's sake, to love your biological mother and your stepmother."

"I wish you'd refer to her as Eleanor," Dean said, a bit sulkily. "She's not my mother, you are."

"Darling Dean, I couldn't love you more if I'd given birth to you, but the fact of the matter is that Eleanor is your mother. She left you, but she didn't renounce you."

"That's just semantics," the boy said importantly. Then, "Why are you taking her side?"

"Are you kidding? I've been in a rage about her since the first day I learned about her. So let me do the raging for us both, okay? That's all I'm saying. Just meet her with your heart open as well as your eyes."

"You think I owe her that?" His mouth curved upward in a lopsided little sneer, which Laurel realized he'd learned from Doug. Good Lord! She hoped he'd unlearn it in a hurry when—if—Doug went on his merry way without them.

"I don't think you owe her anything," Laurel said, "except the common courtesy we all owe everybody. I think it's to yourself that you owe the open heart. There's no such thing as having too many people to love, right?"

"Right," Dean grudgingly agreed. "I think I'll go get a glass of milk. Want anything?"

"No, thanks, honey. I'm heading upstairs. I'm going to read awhile in bed, so just knock if you need to talk about any of this."

A few minutes later, just as she had settled among her pillows and was taking up a collection of Mark Twain stories she'd been meaning to get into for some time, the knock came. Hoping Dean hadn't started to develop anxieties about Eleanor's visit, she called to him to come in.

"I forgot to tell you," he said. "I've been offered a job."

"A job?"

"Well, sort of. I'd be a volunteer, actually, but making money isn't all that counts at a job, is it?"

Solemnly Laurel agreed it wasn't. What was the point of being fake with Dean? He was never going to have to worry about money.

"It's at Camp ICY," Dean said. "Mr. Gladstone said he liked the way I was interacting with John Coover and the other junior campers, and he asked if I'd like to work with that age group during the August session. Sports and stuff. So even if I wanted to, I couldn't go away with Eleanor for more than a week or so because I made a commitment."

Feeling tears prickling her eyelids, Laurel automatically started to put her control mechanisms to work, then remembered that staying in control was no longer the abiding ambition of her life. Sniffling openly, she reached for a tissue.

"What's the matter?" Dean asked. "Did I say something wrong?"

"Not for a minute! I'm crying because I'm so proud and happy about your making a commitment to something. And a very fine commitment it happened to be, if you ask me."

Dean smiled and waved his half-empty glass of milk. "Night, Laurel."

"Night, honey. Don't forget that Mrs. Cunningham is coming in tomorrow."

"So if you want any laundry done, put it in the hamper," he chorused with her, this being their Friday-night litany.

"Fresh kid." Laurel blew him a kiss. "Sweet dreams, honey."

The morning was as clear and bright as her sleep had been serene. Laurel making coffee while Dean squeezed the oranges, they concocted happy scenarios in which Doug performed all sorts of astonishing feats at Falling Water that day.

"How about a shot off the first tee that sails around the dogleg and flies into the cup," Dean suggested.

"That would not only make Falling Water history, I think it would make the *Guinness Book of World Records*," Laurel said. "But if anyone can do it, our Doug can," she added recklessly.

"You know what?" Dean said. "It would actually tie the world record, on the nose, because the yardage from the men's tee is 392 yards, and that's exactly what Tommy Campbell hit in Dublin one year!"

"Hang on," Laurel said, slicing bread for toast. "It's 392 yards from the men's tee, but Doug is playing from the championship tees, remember? That's—what?—410 yards?"

"Yeah, 413," Dean said. "Not too likely, eh? How about an eagle 2?"

"I'm sure he'd be very happy with an eagle 2, and would you mind telling me where you got that Canadian 'eh'?"

"You know where I got it," Dean said. "I think it sounds nice."

"I just hope Doug doesn't think you're making fun of him."

"Oh, he's too smart to think that," Dean said. "Now on the seventeenth hole, how about if his second shot lands in the trap, and everybody's dying, and then he lofts it right out into the cup."

"Be great on a movie screen," Laurel said, "but I don't know if I want to live through the tension of seeing him in the bunker. Well—if you promise me he's out of there and onto the green—"

"Into the cup," Dean insisted.

"Then I guess I can live with it. You want eggs, honey?"

"I'm too excited for eggs. I'm going to have granola."

"Me, too," Laurel decided. "A noisy breakfast."

Wavering between wearing golf clothes and dressing in "civvies," she decided that golf shoes would really be more comfortable than sneakers or sandals for following Doug around the course. She hated the way golf shoes looked with street-length skirts or tailored slacks—definitely an Iron Maiden combination—so she put on a pair of mid-thigh flared khaki culottes, which Doug wouldn't absolutely despise yet which wouldn't cause any ruptured arteries among the club grandees. Passing over the sort of knit golf shirt she knew Doug positively loathed, she donned a blue-and-white checked man-tailored shirt and rolled up the sleeves. Wearing navy flats for the drive to the club, she would change into the blue-and-white golf shoes she'd won after the pro-am event—and hope that their "lucky" properties would work for Doug.

Traffic was so slow between Farmingdale Center and Falling Water she wondered if there had been an accident, then realized that because today was Saturday there would probably be twice as many people attending the Classic as there had been yesterday, and she was in a plain old traffic jam.

"I hope we won't miss Doug at the first tee," she anxiously told Dean.

"He'll insist on waiting for you," Dean teased. "So what if they penalize him a couple of strokes for holding up play? He can afford them."

"Don't get too cocky on his behalf," Laurel warned. "He tied for second place yesterday, which is perfectly fantastic for a rabbit—for anyone; but can he keep it up under pressure? He's a truly great golfer, Dean, but he's not the only great—or ambitious—player out there today."

She knew she meant the words for her own ears as well as Dean's, that she was trying to cushion herself against the possibility of disappointment. She also knew that her hopes for the day were even more extravagant than the boy's. Whether he'd intended to or not, Doug had elevated the Classic to a kind of mythic importance, and had definitely linked it with their relationship. It wasn't that he saw her as part of the winner's swag, something that came with the territory. She'd had her fears in that direction, but he'd pretty much stilled them. No—Doug Stewart wasn't a brute of a man to want a human trophy. It was just that both of them somehow knew if he could win the event against that fine field of competitors, then anything on earth was possible. Even that Doug and she could break their cycle of suspicion and tension long enough to admit that they'd found love—and that running from their emotions was self-defeating.

This morning she felt that she had an inner clarity that rivaled the blazingly bright blue sky. That's what she and Doug had been doing, wasn't it? Running? Wasn't that what the ritual dance of kiss, squabble, kiss, squabble was all about? Thrilling to the unexpected arrival of romance in their lives, yet knowing that it was a ferocious demand on the soul and therefore to be feared? Because if she and Doug made a life together, each was going to be obsessed with the idea of living up to the other's standards and endlessly delighting each other—without betraying their own perhaps very different standards. Yet were they so different? Underneath the differences in style Laurel suspected that there lived two minds with similar standards, two hearts with needs and strengths as confluent as the utterly compatible needs and strengths of their bodies.

If only she could be absolutely sure. If only he would tell her more about himself. A dreadful possibility came to roost in her mind, like some dark, menacing bird. Had he kept her from looking at his passport because he'd been photographed with a woman and child—the love child she could too easily imagine him having? Clare Hamilton, his big buddy, must know all the seamy details—if they *were* seamy. Laurel wouldn't dream of pumping her, but she thought wistfully that she would be awfully happy if the talky reporter slipped her some information.

Sounding nervous, Dean said, "It's almost ten. Should I get out and see how backed up the road is? We're just inching along."

"I know," Laurel moaned. Doug's tee-off time this morning was ten-twenty, and they were still a good fifteen minutes from the club under the best of conditions.

"You could take a shortcut," Dean said.

"You mean Fishermen's Way? Does it still go all the way through to Route 10?"

"Yup," Dean said.

"I don't know," Laurel said doubtfully. Patting the fine-grained wood dashboard of the Mercedes, she added, "This is a great car, but it's not exactly four-wheel drive—and the suspension's pretty low. I'd hate to lose my transmission in the middle of nowhere."

"I've done it in the wagon," Dean said, challengingly. "You just don't believe in shortcuts in the same way you didn't think acupressure could cure your headache yesterday. But it helped, didn't it?"

"I *think* it helped—though maybe it was the aspirin or just knowing how concerned you were." Dean didn't answer. Wanting him to know at this touchy juncture in his life that she believed in him, and not wanting to miss Doug at the first tee as they surely would if she went on crawling along Farmingdale River Road, she said, "All right, let's give it a try. I can get to it just at the top of this hill, can't I?"

Turning onto Fishermen's Way, Laurel realized that the road was even rougher than she'd remembered it. Scarcely wide enough to accommodate a single vehicle, it had a reputation for deep potholes and obtruding branches as well as being the route to the richest trout pools in the area.

"What happens if we meet another car?" she asked Dean. "Does one of us have to ford the river?" A branch from an oak tree reached impudently through the open roof to graze her cheek, and Laurel decided to put up the top. Feeling the car grazing rocks, hearing ominous scraping sounds, she wondered if she hadn't made one of the less intelligent choices of her life when she'd cut out of the maddeningly slow, but reliable Farmingdale Road. But, Lord, it was pretty down here, almost sav-

agely beautiful, with the lush greens of the overgrown
bushes and unchecked trees, highlighted by the occasional pink and purple of mountain laurel and azalea.
The Farmingdale River, to their right, was a gently ed-
dying translucent blue, revealing mossy patches and
pleasingly irregular rock formations. Some of the pools
had names—Rainbow Pool, Heartbreak Hole, Anglers'
Agony, Frog Hollow—according to the fishing lore as-
sociated with each one.

Though she rarely thought back to her childhood, one
of the memories she cherished was of a trout fishing
expedition with her Uncle Jack and two of her boy cousins. The boys had quickly grown impatient, but she'd
delighted her uncle with her willingness to cast and cast
again and her interest in knowing the names of all the
different dry flies and lures and understanding why one
used a Nymph here, an Irresistible there. Her reward had
been the satisfaction of hooking and landing a twelve-
inch brown trout, and proudly presenting it to Aunt Bett,
who had gutted it and sautéed it and served it with much
ceremony at dinnertime, making sure everyone in the
family got a taste.

Those boy cousins of hers had boys of their own
now—one of them about John Coover's age. Laurel
found herself wishing that she'd done a better job of
staying in touch with her adoptive family, scattered
though they were across the country. Letters and presents
were exchanged at Christmastime, and she had a tickler
file to remind her of her nieces' and nephews' birthdays,
but she didn't really *know* any of them, and suddenly she
felt a loss. She drifted off into a fantasy of a big wedding,
with her family gathering from near and far to see her
and Doug walk hand in hand down the eighteenth fairway, toward the perfectly manicured green and the waiting minister. But golf shoes with a wedding dress? Even
though she wouldn't be wearing a young virgin's white
lace, she—

"Laurel, look out!"

Coming back to reality, she jammed on her brakes as a magnificent buck deer bounded across the road from the direction of the river and vanished into the woods.

"Are there really deer down here?" she exclaimed, as though she doubted her eyes.

"Lots of deer. And pheasant, rabbits, racoons—I've even seen wild turkeys and foxes here."

"Why didn't you share this with me?" Laurel asked, teasingly.

"What's to win?" Dean asked.

"What do you mean?" She winced as she heard a scraping noise alongside the car, though she'd happily pay for a new paint job if the shortcut worked.

"You always said you only liked competitive sports— so it was pretty pointless to invite you to go hiking or fishing. You seemed to think I was trying to escape something when I took to the woods."

Laurel let out a little groan. "Was I really that narrow-minded?" she asked, feeling as if they were discussing another person, not herself.

"Yup," Dean said cheerfully.

Dividing the world up into winners and losers. Doug had seen that trait in her, had spotted it during the torrid first encounter on the practice tee. She wasn't about to renounce her love of competitive sports, but had she perhaps carried that love over into areas of life where it didn't belong? Was that why there had been so much strife between her and Doug, because she harbored the notion that only one of them could be victorious in their relationship?

"Hey, there's Route 10!" Dean exclaimed.

Glancing at the clock on the dashboard, Laurel realized that, barring calamity, they would make it to the club on time. "The shortcut was an inspired idea," she told her stepson. "And let's go fishing one of these days, okay?"

"Do you think Doug would like to come fishing with us?" Dean asked.

"Damn it," Laurel said happily, "I do wish you two would stop reading my mind!"

chapter

10

GENTLY ELBOWING A path to the forefront of Doug's gallery at the first tee, Laurel decided that the warmth of his expression as he looked at her and Dean more than compensated for the nerve-wracking drive and the assault on the finish of the Mercedes. Her heart soared as he drew his driver back in that great big swing of his, and her hips ached sweetly with a longing to move in tandem with his pivoting hips. Applauding with the rest of the enthusiastic crowd, she turned to Dean and remarked that the curving, powerhouse drive was almost as brilliant as the *Guinness* record-breaking tee-shot that the two of them had conjured in their breakfasttime fantasy.

"Darling, you know how to pick them!" Elsie Howard said to Laurel, as they walked along the rough bordering the first fairway. "I think your rabbit is going to leave here sixty thousand dollars richer." Hearing Laurel sigh, Elsie gave her friend a long look and said, "You're not so happy about the leaving here part, are you?"

Mulling her reply, Laurel overheard one of Webb Daniels's gambling friends mutter to another, "The rabbit's hot. A C-spot says he breaks the course record today."

"He's good—but I don't know if he's that good," the second man answered. "It's a bet."

Laurel froze. Sensing that Dean's reaction was similar to her own, she put an arm around his shoulders but didn't dare say anything.

The course record! She loved the idea of Doug outdriving the *Guinness* record holder, and she dearly wanted him to win the Southern New England Classic, but did she want him to break the Falling Water course record?

A dozen years ago, Reed Campion had shot a ten-under-par 62 for a new course low, and neither pro nor amateur had ever bettered that score.

Doug Stewart had carried her to unprecedented heights of sensual ecstasy, and impulsively she'd blurted out the truth in bed, telling him that he'd broken a course record. Did she want him to take away all of Reed's trophies?

"Records are made to be broken, my darlings," the ever-perceptive Elsie said to Laurel and Dean.

"I know one thing," Dean commented fiercely. "Nobody *except* Doug better beat Dad's record."

Laurel laughed and gave him a hug. "We should all have your perspective on life, Dean."

Doug didn't break any records on the first hole, but he did sink a longish putt for a birdie 3, turning to wink broadly at Laurel and Dean as his caddy retrieved the ball from the cup. Pressing on toward the second tee, Laurel took her thoughts from Doug long enough to marvel at the size and expectant mood of the crowd. Like so many exotic insects in their bright summer garb, men, women, and children were swarming over the rises, pressing against the marshals' ropes. They were quick to applaud, and they were capable of holding their collective breath and all but ceasing to move when a player addressed the ball. Even babes in backpacks seemed to understand that one didn't so much as gurgle during a putt, and Laurel was unable to fend off a brief but searing fantasy in which Doug was playing in the Masters', and she was the one with the baby—their baby—in a backpack.

Adding to the festivities and heightening the tension were the television crews with their portable video equipment. Several of the superstar sportscasters were waxing knowledgeable into their miniature microphones. Laurel saw Clare Hamilton in animated discussion with colleagues on the sporting press who were no doubt trying to pump her for inside information on the hot rabbit out of Toronto. Wishing she, too, dared pump Clare for the scoop on Doug Stewart, Laurel contented herself with an animated exchange of waves.

Laurel had been hoping to discuss the impending visit of Eleanor Ligeret with Elsie, but she didn't want to bring the subject up in front of Dean. It was a relief when Dean himself turned to Elsie and said, "Did Eleanor— my mother—play golf, Mrs. Howard? She's coming to visit tomorrow."

"I know she is," Elsie replied gravely. "I don't think she was ever much of an athlete, Dean. Swam a little, maybe."

"How about stuff like hiking and fishing?"

Recognizing that the contractions in her stomach were signaling the shameful presence of jealousy, Laurel turned away, pretending interest in a pair of cardinals chattering high up in a maple tree.

"I suppose she could have changed," Elsie responded, "but the Eleanor I knew wasn't interested in any activities that required wearing what she regarded as unfeminine clothes."

"Then what did she wear to paint?" Dean asked, with his blunt teenage practicality.

"Pretty peasant-type dresses under flowing white smocks," Elsie said, not censoring the tartness in her voice. "What did she care? She didn't have to do the laundry. Sorry, darling," she added. "I'm afraid I'm being tactless as all get out. In her own way, Eleanor was a rather fascinating woman, and certainly a beautiful one. But she never knew her own heart, and that can wreck the hooey out of a life—*and* other people's lives."

"You mean she shouldn't have had me?"

"I don't mean that for a minute, silly boy. I meant—" Her round cheeks flaming, she added lamely, "Well, it doesn't really matter what I meant. You're just going to have to make up your own mind about her, aren't you?"

"I've already made up my mind about everything," Dean said, looking up at Laurel. "I'm going to try to like Eleanor, but I'm staying with Laurel."

"That's what I call sound thinking all around," Elsie said, clearly relieved to be off the hook. "Now how is Doug going to play that one?" she wailed, as his approach shot to the third green landed in the steep trap that always made Laurel think of a fried egg perched on edge.

"He's going to blast it the hell out of there," Laurel said, her calm voice belying her anxiety. Looking down at the shoes she'd won, as though to remind them that they were supposed to convey luck to Doug, she tried to think herself into the sand wedge in Doug's hands, the way she did when she had to get herself out of the bunker—tried to direct her mind to the sweet spot, and the sweet spot to the ball.

A chorus of gasps and loud applause told her that Doug had played the shot beautifully, and she raised her eyes to see the ball sitting, in all its orange impudence, an easy two feet from the cup.

After Doug had sunk his putt for his third consecutive birdie of the morning, he turned toward the crowd as if searching for someone. Then, when his eyes found Laurel's face, he mouthed a word.

"What?" she mouthed back.

"Thanks," she read.

Shivering a little, she wondered if he were thanking her for her help in playing the shot. But that was mystical nonsense, wasn't it? It was one thing to focus all your concentration on the club—another matter altogether to believe your mind could influence another person's shot, for better or for worse. When Dean had been in his meditation phase, they'd had some strong arguments on the subject. Oh, Lord, was she going to have second thoughts about everything on earth before she and Doug Stewart were done with each other?

Insisting inwardly that she was merely indulging herself, she tried to think herself into the sweet spot every time Doug raised his club, with the astonishing result— or, rather, she corrected herself, the astonishing coincidence—that he got two more birdies. On the easy par 3 sixth hole, she deliberately turned her mind to mundane matters—reminding herself that she'd run out of juice oranges, making a mental note to ask Pete Howard about a fishing lodge he'd gone to in Maine, possibly a nice place to take Dean to celebrate his eighteenth birthday. To her dismay, Doug shanked his tee shot into the rough, hit an indifferent nine iron that limped onto the green, then proceeded to two-putt—for a bogie 4! Was her imagination working overtime, or was he giving her a look that scolded her for letting him down?

She "helped" him on the next three holes, and at the end of the front nine his score stood at an amazing 31— five under par. The day Reed had set the course record, his score on the front nine had been 32. The hot rabbit from Toronto had already burned a record, and the gallery was jubilant.

Pete Howard, with an eight-year-old child hanging onto each hand, joined Elsie, Laurel, and Dean at the tenth tee. Little Tony and Tracy Howard watched raptly as Doug hit a soaring three-hundred-yard drive, and then announced that they'd seen enough golf. Could Dean please take them to one of the tents and buy them popcorn?

"Hey, kids, you just got here," Pete protested. "Anyway, Dean wants to watch the action."

"I don't see any action," eight-year-old Tracy said innocently.

"The players have to walk between their shots, darling," Elsie began, then gave up with a little smile. "It's not exactly like watching the World Series, is it? Tell you what. I'll take you for popcorn. One small popcorn, which you will share."

"That's okay, Mrs. Howard. I'll take them," Dean said.

"You sure?" Pete said. He produced a dollar bill from a pants pocket.

"Nope, my treat, Dr. Howard," Dean insisted.

"He's turning into quite a young man," Elsie said, as Dean walked off with her children.

"He got asked to be a counselor at Camp ICY," Laurel announced proudly. "I think he wanted to take Tony and Tracy to get in a little practice."

"Laurel, I know how you feel about kids showing respect for us geriatric folk," Pete said, as they drew abreast of Doug's ball, "but I think it's high time he dropped this 'Dr.' and 'Mrs.' nonsense and called us Pete and—what's your name, dear?"

"Dulcinea," Elsie answered prettily. "Do you come here often?" Linking arms with her husband, she said to Laurel, "He's right, darling. Dean's growing up. By the way, I—"

"Shh," Laurel said, holding up her head, turning away to be with Doug in spirit as he took an eight iron from his caddy and shifted into his wide stance. For a sublime, dizzying moment, Laurel felt as if she were having one of those out-of-body experiences Dean liked to talk about now and then . . . as if her actual substance was merging with Doug's even though yards of space separated their shells. It wasn't just that her hands were on the club with his: his hands were her hands, and her hands were his. All boundaries between them were vanishing, as they had when they lay entwined in her bed, losing themselves and finding each other—finding everything they needed.

His ball took flight, and she was released, a delicate tingling in her breasts the only memento of the sublime moment. Drawing breath, flashing an apologetic little grin at Elsie, she said, "Sorry, Els. What were you saying? About Dean?"

"Only that I could have strangled myself for letting the cat out of the bag. You know," at Laurel's blank look, "about Eleanor."

"What cat out of what bag?" Laurel returned. "Dean knows everything there is to know, doesn't he?"

"I'm not sure he does," Elsie said. "I'm not sure you do, either, darling, and I think it's high time you did."

"Did you know," Elsie began, "that Eleanor wanted to take Dean with her when she fled to the south of France?"

"What?" Laurel exclaimed.

"I *thought* you didn't know," Elsie said grimly. "Heaven knows, I tried to bring up the subject of Eleanor often enough, but even after Reed died you seemed to think it was disloyal to him to discuss her."

"Now, wait a minute," Pete Howard interjected. "Eleanor *said* she wanted to take Dean with her, but she was certainly talked out of it easily enough. I think she was just saying what she thought she should say, Elsie. Giving lip service to the maternal bond, and all that. It didn't seem to take Reed more than five minutes—and one whopping big financial settlement—to persuade her that she owed it to her son to let him be brought up with all the comforts of Farmingdale."

"Please," Laurel implored. "Reed wasn't the kind of man to try to separate a mother and child, for any reason."

"Don't be so touchy, darling," Elsie said, brushing back her thick, dark bangs. "I'm not attacking Reed, for the love of Mike. For sure, whatever he did he thought it was the right thing to do, and it probably was. Look. It's simply that the moment came when Eleanor felt she could no longer live in Farmingdale and live the Falling Water life. She'd grown up in Greenwich Village, gone to art school, and though her feeling for Reed had gotten her through the first few years of life here, she was suddenly suffocating. Really on the edge of a breakdown, I think."

"Baloney," Pete exploded. "She was a selfish—"

"Hush up," Elsie said. "Let me finish. The marriage had been stormy at best, and I don't think Reed was devastated by the thought of divorce. But losing his boy was another question. I think he figured Dean needed a father as much as he needed a mother, and that he was at least as likely to do a good job of being a parent as Eleanor was. So he told Eleanor if she wanted to go paint in her beloved south of France, he'd stake her to a more than comfortable existence—if she left Dean behind. But if she fought for custody of Dean, he would make sure first of all that a court order kept her in Connecticut, and second, though he would make sure the boy never wanted for anything, that she would have to fight for every nickel of alimony."

"Elsie Howard, for someone who is usually the most sensible woman on God's earth, you somehow managed to let that self-important, self-involved Eleanor convince you that Reed did something wrong in putting pressure on Eleanor to leave Dean behind." Pete gave an exasperated little sigh and took out his pipe. "Didn't Dean have a wonderful upbringing?"

"Yes, of course," Elsie quickly conceded, "but was it quite fair of Reed to let Dean grow up thinking that his mother really had no interest in him at all and saw him as an impediment to her painting?"

"Oh, now, Elsie," Pete said, lighting up, "Reed never made her sound that evil. After all, she did put her self-fulfillment above Dean's well-being."

"Please," Laurel begged. "Please."

"I'm sorry," Elsie said contritely. "This is hardly the time or place. But with Eleanor coming tomorrow—"

"I'm glad you told me," Laurel said. "It's just that Dean adored Reed so, and I hate the idea of his image of Reed being shattered—"

"Reed did the right thing, damn it!" Pete boomed. "Dean ought to be proud that his father was willing to do anything to keep him."

"Yes, but Reed should have told him the truth. And now," Laurel added unhappily, "I'm going to do my best to keep the truth from him. Who else knows? Sara? Evan? They certainly won't say a word against Reed. I suppose Webb knows. He can be counted on. Where is Webb, anyway? Following Jack Nicklaus around? I thought he was getting to like Doug, and—" Her voice trailed off as a movement on the course caught her eye. "Elsie! What's Doug doing?"

Craning, Elsie said, "He's brushing something away from the apron."

Her voice panicky, Laurel said, "He's not brushing away sand, is he? It looks a little like sand."

"Hey, calm down, darling," Elsie said. "I'm sure he knows the rules as well as you do. He wouldn't brush away anything unless it was artificial. But it does look like sand," she agreed unhappily.

"Oh, no," Laurel moaned. There was a buzz growing among the press people, indicating that other people believed Doug might have violated the rule against moving "loose impediments," a phrase denoting natural objects, including sand. "One stroke could make all the difference!"

"I'm afraid it's a two-stroke penalty, darling," Elsie said, as a PGA official started across the fairway to confer with Doug and his caddy. Bending to examine the ground around Doug's ball, the official seemed to be nodding in agreement with Doug, then stood up and walked back to the TV announcers, a perplexed look on his face.

The word quickly got back to Laurel, Elsie, and Pete that the substance in question wasn't sand, it was popcorn—apparently dropped by a careless spectator and blown onto the course by the wind. Corn was natural—but was popcorn? Or did the fact that it had undergone processing mean that it was an "artificial obstruction" rather than a "loose impediment," and therefore removable from the line of play without penalty?

While the official went to the committee tent to get a ruling, Doug played out the hole, getting par despite the tension surrounding him, and despite Laurel's momentary mental paralysis.

"A wooden match stick is an artificial obstruction even though a splinter of wood is a loose impediment, right?" she babbled at Elsie.

"Right," Elsie agreed.

"Then again," Laurel said, her famously steady voice tremulous, "a match has had a sulfur head put on it, and you can't say that about popcorn. Do you suppose," she said, near-hysterical giggles bubbling under her words, "that the decision will hinge on whether the popcorn was buttered? Or whether it has artificial preservatives in it?"

"It's one for the books, for sure!" Elsie said.

As Dean came threading his way through the crowd with Tracy and Tony Howard, Laurel took one look at the cardboard box of popcorn and let out a loud groan.

"What's the matter?" Dean asked.

"The box says 'all natural.'"

"You mean you'd rather have the kids eat popcorn with artificial flavoring and coloring?" Dean asked. Scratching his head, he said, "I know you think I'm a nut on the subject of natural foods, but that doesn't mean there's something wrong with popcorn that doesn't—"

"I know, I know," Laurel said. "It's just that—" And she explained about Doug's dilemma.

As Doug was about to tee up on the twelfth hole, the word came through from the committee. Popcorn—even "all natural" popcorn—was an artificial obstruction and Doug had been within his rights to remove it from the apron. A cheer went up from the crowd, and a broadly grinning Doug responded by belting the ball clear across the steep-sided gurgling brook.

Had it been only two days ago, Laurel thought dreamily, that all hell had broken loose in the skies over the lush fairway—and the Epsteins' barn, just visible from where she now stood, had turned out to be the gateway to heaven? Heat rushing through her veins as she relived the ecstasy of lying in Doug's arms, she followed the crowd down a path to the right of the fairway. Oh, when would their lips meet again, their bodies entwine once more? Would she ever know the joy of waking up beside him? Dreamily, she imagined waking at dawn to bird songs while Doug slept on, and she saw herself gently, almost tentatively, flicking her tongue along his earlobes...the corners of his mouth...the underside of his strong jaw....traveling downward to dance through the thicket of hair on his chest and still further downward, until he emerged from sleep, calling out her name and his desire for her.

Birdieing the twelfth hole, Doug gave the impression of a man who simply could not be stopped. As players who had teed off ahead of him finished their rounds, reports filtered back to Doug's gallery of some very creditable scores: a 6 under par for one of the big-name pros, a 7 under par for a twenty-year-old amateur from nearby Wampannoag Country Club who had played Falling Water many times. But Doug could beat any of them.

Frankly dazed by the time Doug was teeing off on the eighteenth hole, Laurel clutched Dean's hand. "Well, baby?" she asked.

"He's something else, isn't he?" Dean said. Coloring slightly, he added, "He's doing it for you, isn't he?"

"He's doing it because it's there," Laurel answered.

"Well, you're more there than there," Dean persisted, "if you know what I mean."

"Sort of," Laurel said. Shading her eyes to track the flight of the perfectly struck drive, she added, "He's doing it for you, too, kiddo. He likes us."

"Do you want him to break Dad's record?" Dean asked quietly. "It's okay if you do."

"Is it?"

"Because I was thinking—even if Doug does break it, Dad will still hold the record for an amateur. I mean, there doesn't always only have to be one winner, does there? I can have two mothers . . . and there can be two course record holders."

"And it's not as if Doug were out there trying to outdo your father," Laurel said. "His caddy probably hasn't even told him what the course record is, let alone who holds it, for fear of unnerving him."

As Doug knelt down on the green to line up the putt on which everything hung, the very wind seemed to stop its whispering, the trees to hold their breath.

Putting his lips to Laurel's ear, Dean said, "Will it in for him, Laurel. It's okay."

"Mystical nonsense," she mouthed; but she willed the putt in with all her heart. As the ball headed straight for the cup and disappeared over the rim, she threw her arms around Dean and joined him in an exuberant scream.

chapter

11

DINNER PARTIES HAD never been Laurel's favorite social event, and if ever there was a particular party she didn't want to be going to on a particular evening, this was it. The hosts were Sara and Evan Campion; the guests were Laurel and Dean and Dean's mother.

"A pride of Campions? A gaggle of Campions?" she murmured, as she and Dean drove through Farmingdale Center.

"What?" Dean asked.

"You know. A pride of lions, a gaggle of geese, a covey of quail, a herd of buffalo—what do you have when you have a multitude of Campions?"

"A pack?" Dean suggested, tagging on a good imitation of a snarl.

"Fun-ny."

"Look," Dean said, as they passed the village green, with its pristine white church and white-trimmed brick library, "there's Ginny. Will you toot?"

Laurel obediently beeped her horn at the snub-nosed redhead. As the Mercedes slowed to a stop at Farmingdale's one traffic signal, Ginny came running across the green and hung on Dean's window.

"You going to the clambake?" Ginny asked.

"Nope. We're going to my aunt and uncle's. You going to the clambake?"

"Sure am."

"Well, eat a dozen ears of corn for me," Dean said.

"Will do. Bye," Ginny said, as the light turned green. "Bye, Mrs. Campion."

"Nice girl," Laurel observed.

"She's okay," Dean said, his casual words at odds with his big grin and heightened color.

As they drove past Wheels 'n' Deals, where Laurel and Reed had once bought Dean a racing bike, and Upper Crust, where every Farmingdale birthday cake was baked, Laurel said to Dean, "Do you like small-town life? Knowing everybody and everybody knowing you?"

"I think I do," Dean said. "Though Ginny's been talking about going to college in New York or Boston, and that sounded kind of interesting."

"Maybe we ought to start poking around some campuses," Laurel said. "In the early fall, before the pressure is on. We could go to the theater, too, eat at exotic restaurants—" She stopped, not wanting to sound as though she were bribing Dean in advance of his meeting with his mother.

"I'd like that," Dean said. Then, a little nervously, he asked, "How do I look?"

"Terrific!" Though she had pointedly refrained from making suggestions to him about how to dress for the evening, Dean had put on a khaki suit, a blue-and-white striped shirt, and a navy tie with red hearts on it. "Didn't you notice Ginny's admiring glances?"

"She only cares about my soul," Dean said.

Something about the sardonic way he cast the phrase made Laurel think about Doug—not that he'd ever been very far from the forefront of her mind since they'd met. She'd insisted that he go to the clambake being held at Falling Water—how could he leave New England without tasting the tender sweet corn and juicy native tomatoes, not to mention the incomparable taste of clams steamed over seaweed? Saying that Laurel was the only juicy native tomato he was really interested in, and that he would gladly see her and Dean through the encounter with Eleanor, he had finally agreed to go to the clambake—on the condition that Laurel meet him there later.

She was half sorry that she hadn't taken him up on his initial offer, but she'd felt that dinner at the Campions would be emotional enough without introducing an extra factor. Besides, what Laurel considered to be Sara's anti-sensuality definitely extended to her kitchen. A succession of cooks over the years had turned out gray roasts and limp vegetables, to the apparent satisfaction of Sara and the dismay of her guests.

Laurel didn't know why she'd thought of Eleanor as a full-bodied woman—maybe because of Elsie's description of her in puff-sleeved, wide-skirted peasant dresses; but Eleanor's slight, almost fragile, build surprised her, and somehow made the "other woman" hard to view as the enemy. Eleanor had brought the rich, ruby-colored wine of her husband's native Nuits-St. Georges with her, and Evan's quick hand with a bottle also facilitated the thawing process in the green and ivory living room. Most of all, Laurel appreciated that Eleanor neither wept nor tore her hair nor beat her bosom nor called Dean "my precious little baby," each of which discomfiting acts Laurel had half-expected. As Sara was dishing out a rather dull-looking apple cake for dessert, Laurel realized that Eleanor had still said nothing remotely possessive about her intentions where Dean was concerned. Perhaps she feared to upset the assembled company's digestive processes?

They were back in the living room and Evan was offering around cognac, when Eleanor smoothed the skirt of her simple violet silk dress, and said, "I'd like you to see my paintings, Dean." Steeling herself to hear Eleanor follow up the comment with an invitation to her studio in the south of France, Laurel was astonished to hear Eleanor add, "This afternoon I was able to make arrangements for a gallery in New York to include me in their stable. As soon as I get back to Juan-les-Pins, I plan to have a number of my oils crated and shipped over to the gallery, and perhaps you and Laurel would find it amusing to go to Soho to see them." Stretching her arms far apart, she said, "My canvases are big, big, big. And very bold. I think they might appeal to a young man like you."

"I'd certainly like to see them," Dean said. "Laurel and I have been talking about going to New York."

"We must all go see them," Evan boomed, raising his snifter in salute to New York or art or perhaps, Laurel thought, the Campion "we."

"We must," echoed Sara, who had been on her best behavior all evening—almost meek in her deference to Laurel.

Sticking to a plan prearranged with Dean, Laurel made her excuses after a few sips of the heady cognac, saying she felt absolutely obligated to drop in at the clambake at Falling Water. A downhill slide of Sara's mouth indicated that she knew perfectly well why Laurel wanted to go to Falling Water that evening, but she refrained from making one of her acid comments and actually seemed to be making an effort to draw her mouth back up into a smile."

"I'll be glad to drive Dean home," Evan boomed.

"Or I can walk," Dean chimed in. "It's a beautiful night."

Seeing Laurel to her car after the amenities were done with, he said, "Wow. It's all so different from what I'd expected."

"Isn't it?" Laurel agreed.

"She's nice," Dean said, "but—I don't know—I just don't feel as though she's my mother. Or that she even wants to be. That's the part I don't get. I really can't believe she came here to take me away with her, unless it's that she decided after an hour with me that I'm not such hot stuff."

"Dean Campion," Laurel began threateningly, "if you don't take that back immediately—"

"I was just kidding."

"Are you disappointed, babe?" Laurel asked, propping herself against the Mercedes and looking at him. "Had you envisioned some lovely Hollywood kind of fight in which she and I would take to the mat and start screaming about who was going to have you?"

"No!" Dean said explosively, leaving Laurel no room for doubt. "I'm only staying now because I agreed with you before that she and I should have a chance to talk privately—and because she's this nice, slightly sad person and I—" Spreading his hands, he looked eloquently at Laurel.

"I understand," she said softly, knowing he wanted to make Eleanor feel important but had too much delicacy to say so. What a boy he was! What a young man! Whatever happened between her and Doug Stewart, she decided, she would always look back on the Southern New England Classic as a watershed event for Dean. Or was she the one who had changed, needing the shock of her encounter with Doug—and her encounter with herself—to appreciate Dean's special qualities? A little of both, she decided.

"Promise me you'll walk home instead of letting Uncle Ev give you a lift if he—"

"Gets soused?" Dean completed cheerfully. "Absolutely. You don't have to worry your sweet little old gray head, Mama."

"Fresh kid," she smiled, opening her car door.

"I do wish Uncle Ev would stop drinking," Dean said with a little sigh and a shrug. "I like him."

"I do, too," Laurel said. An idea she'd reminded herself to think about at a future date surfaced in her mind, and she added, "I have a notion that might just help. It has to do with ICY kids and golf. Tell you about it later, okay?"

Driving toward Falling Water, Laurel decided on sudden impulse to stop by her house and change her clothes. She'd chosen a pretty, but decidedly unexciting, high-necked, silk print dress to wear to Sara and Evan's, and decidedly unexciting was hardly the way she wanted to appear to Doug Stewart. Browsing critically through her closet, she decided to wear the blue, green, and violet chiffon dress with spaghetti straps and softly swirling skirt that she'd worn the other night. Let Doug know that she dressed for his eyes, and that she didn't care if the people of Falling Water saw her in the same dress at two consecutive club parties.

Shucking the bra she wouldn't need under the fitted bodice of the dress, Laurel moaned as she remembered how fantastically alive her nipples had felt when Doug had caressed them through the fabric of the dress. Quickly putting on her lavender sandals, she got back into her car and headed for the club as fast as the speed limit would allow.

All was quiet at the temporary admissions gate that had been erected for the Classic, but bursts of jug-band music and the sounds of social merriment came from the stretch of lawn between the clubhouse and the ninth green, the stretch which had come to be known as "the beach" because it was the site of the club's popular monthly clambakes. Because the pros playing in the Classic had been invited to attend this particular clambake, the membership had turned out in force. Under gaily swaying Japanese lanterns and a moon just shy of full, Laurel saw young and old eating, drinking, talking animatedly, and dancing.

But where was Doug?

Noticing the way the young college women were clustering around the pros, Laurel couldn't help feeling a twinge of anxiety. Sex was very definitely in the air, with the handsome, tanned, younger pros frankly eyeing the pretty girls in their fashionable knickers and culottes and strapless gauze cotton dresses. Doug was not only to her mind, more attractive than the conventionally handsome pros, he was the star of the day, and if he wanted groupies to affirm his status, he could probably have his pick of the lot.

Where was Doug—and where was Lucy Webster, with whom he'd danced the other evening and who had offered him a ride back to his hotel?

"Isn't the rabbit divine?" she heard one young woman murmur to another.

"Yes, those hazel eyes, and that sexy voice of his, *eh?*" the second young woman said.

"Oh, but look, there's Kevin Cohn," the first young woman said, excitedly, pointing out the amateur from nearby Wampannnoag Country Club who had been second low on the course that day, with an eight-under-par 64. "Let's go get him!"

Turning away in disgust, Laurel chided herself for being a prude and a hypocrite. She had gotten down to basics with Doug Stewart pretty quickly herself!

Yes—but she *loved* him. He hadn't been a diversion, a trophy, a flag to wave under the noses of the Falling Water grandees—no matter what he may have thought to the contrary.

Seeing Elsie and Pete dancing with a blissful air appropriate to newlyweds, Laurel felt sheer envy stab at her. If anyone deserved simple happiness it was they, but she couldn't help contrasting her unresolved state with theirs. Would she and Doug ever know each other well enough, trust each other enough, to be a true couple?

Even Webb Daniels, coming toward her her with a giddy Clare Hamilton, emanated a kind of smugness and contentment for which she would have gladly traded her house, car, and famous ability to hit out of the rough.

Gesturing toward her laden plate, the pixieish Clare said, "I've never eaten anything like this sweet corn. Webb says there's a strain called Silver Queen that doesn't ripen until September and is even more delicious, and he's promised to buy me all I can eat if I come back here some weekend. After all, corn is my middle name, eh?"

Groaning, Webb said, "I've changed my mind. I'll just ship some Silver Queen up to you."

"After all that line you were feeding me about how you have to have the water boiling before you pick the corn if you want to taste it at its best? Oh, no, my Connecticut Yankee, you're not getting off so easily."

"How did the great reunion go?" Webb asked Laurel, lightly putting a hand on one of Clare's shoulders.

"Much easier than Dean or I thought it would. Either Eleanor had a change of heart, or Sara somehow misunderstood her intentions, but she seemed very much to be a woman who wanted to get to know Dean a little and wanted him to know her a little but wasn't trying to stake any claim. Unless—" A thought crossing her mind, she said, "Webb, why weren't you at the Classic today?"

"Oh, ah, I had pressing business."

"In New York?" Laurel probed.

"Maybe," he said, running fingers through his gray hair, smiling slightly.

"Maybe using your famous connections to get a certain artist's work into a New York gallery in exchange for her agreeing to drop certain plans of hers?"

"You wouldn't want me to violate a client's privilege," Webb said, in his most lawyerlike voice.

"Client nothing, you old darling!"

"It was the least—"

A giddy shout intruded, and Laurel turned to see a breathless Lucy Webster, her luxurious chestnut hair bouncing behind her, waving a pair of jeans and shouting, "I got them! I got them!"

As Lucy's contemporaries came running toward their giddy friend, Laurel realized with a great thud of her heart that the jeans were unmistakably one of the faded pair that Doug Stewart favored. Oh, Lord, yes, she had seen his hands at the buckle of that hand-tooled leather belt—oh, pain and agony!

Lucy was giggling and saying, "It was easy!" Holding the jeans to her cheek with an intimate little look Laurel found positively nauseating, Lucy said, "Anyone want to hear the gory details?"

"What's that all about?" Clare said.

"I haven't the faintest idea," Laurel said, calling on all her practiced coolness to project an air of indifference.

"This reporter's curiosity is piqued," Clare said. "I think there may be a nice little human-interest sidebar here."

"You know, I'm just not used to going a whole Saturday without swinging a golf club," Laurel declared. "I'm going to hit off a bucket."

Trusting that she looked as though she had nothing on her mind but exercise, she ran off toward the clubhouse to change into golf clothes. What a fool she'd been to dress to please Doug Stewart that night. What a fool she'd been about everything. He—

He was coming toward her, fully dressed, impeccably

dressed, in yet another handsome, summerweight sport coat—this one a blue and white plaid—and crisp, cuffed, white slacks!

"Darling!" he exclaimed, a smile chasing away his scowl.

"But I thought—"

"You thought what? Lord, you look gorgeous. I'm so glad you wore that dress." Crushing her to him, he murmured sweet nothings into her hair, then brought his lips crashing down on hers in a kiss that all but brought her to her knees in pure pleasure. "Thought what?" he went on, a glorious eternity later.

"I thought—" Laughter of relief and exhilaration bubbling up, Laurel managed to say, "I thought you were lying on a green somewhere, waiting for Lucy Webster to bring back your jeans!"

"So she's the little rat!" Doug thundered.

"You mean—"

"Not what you think, you sin-obsessed New Englander." Ruffling Laurel's hair, plainly not angry at her, he explained, "Murph Michaels told me I could leave a change in his locker this evening, in case I wanted to hit off a bucket. Which is exactly what I was about to do, since I was going crazy waiting for you to show up. When I got to Murph's locker, I discovered that my jeans were gone, and one of the men told me he thought he'd seen a girl sneak into the locker room and snatch something. Murph's locker is right near the door, so it wouldn't be all that hard. I ought to tan her fanny, eh?"

"Don't you dare!" Laurel said. "She'd love nothing more!" Returning his fond smile, she said, "I was on my way to practice, too."

"Two minds with a single thought, eh? What do you say we go practice our kissing instead?"

"You mean you think my technique needs work?" Laurel asked, pretending to pout.

"I think your technique is perfection itself," Doug

said. "But even the best of us has to keep practicing and taking lessons, eh?"

"True," Laurel admitted.

Arm in arm they wandered away from the crowd and the clubhouse, toward the moon-washed, deserted eighteenth green. Departing from their fantasy long enough to ask about Dean and hear the reassuring news, Doug then said to Laurel, "We've gone minutes without a fight. Are you bored?"

"I've been more bored in my life."

Slipping off her high-heeled sandal, which would have punctured the flawless-looking surface, Laurel followed Doug onto the eighteenth green.

"Now the first thing you need to know," Doug said, in his teaching pro's voice, "is the importance of assuming a closed stance before beginning the kiss."

Standing with her feet close together, Laurel said, "Like this?"

"That's right." Gathering her into his arms, letting her feel the hardness of his body against hers, he said, "The closed stance permits the two competitors—er, partners—to have maximum contact."

"I see what you mean," Laurel said, a little breathlessly.

"Now comes the all-important question of the grip," Doug said, running his hands up and down Laurel's bare arms, provoking shivers of delight. "Since your partner is taller than you are, I think you might to good advantage reach up and clasp your hands at the back of his neck, pulling his head slightly down toward yours."

"Like this?" Laurel asked, reaching.

"Excellent," Doug said, clasping his own hands behind her back.

"But my wrists don't seem to stay straight, teacher," Laurel murmured, as her hands wandered into his sandy hair as if by their own accord. Behind him, the red flag with its numerals was shimmering in the moonlight, and the course swelled and dipped, seeming to disappear into a horizon of dark trees.

"I suppose there's a time for everything in life, even unstraight wrists," Doug conceded. His mouth mere millimeters from hers now, so that the sweetness of his breath was in her nostrils, he said, "And now the lips."

"The lips," Laurel echoed.

"For lips there is also the question of the closed stance versus the open stance, and my school of thought very strongly favors the open stance."

"I think I can see your point of view," Laurel managed to say, as she reveled in the sweet torment of having his mouth so near hers yet not quite touching it.

Then their parted lips joined, and her whole body surged as electrical currents sizzled through her veins. Their mouths moving frantically, as though to consume one another, Laurel and Doug sank slowly to the silken emerald cushion of the green.

Staring up at the starry sky and at the waxing moon, Laurel felt as if the very universe were conferring its blessings on the twosome of D. Stewart and L. Campion. Pulling Doug's hands to her breasts, she murmured, "Do you mind if we play winter rules and I improve your lie?"

"Sorry," Doug answered tenderly, "but standards are standards. Two stroke penalty. Is there some part of your magnificent body you particularly want stroked?"

"You know where I want to be stroked. Oh," she gasped, as his hands moved possessively over her, "breaking the rules really pays around here."

"Are you mine, Laurel? Are you truly mine? On fairway and on rough? On the eagle holes and the double bogies, too?"

"Even if you whiff and slice and shank and remove loose impediments from the hazard, I am yours."

chapter

12

EARLY SUNDAY MORNING Laurel threw a light wrapper over her nightgown, tiptoed past Dean's room and down the stairs, opened the front door, happily noted the clear sky and moderate temperature, and retrieved the *Hartford Courant* from her front stoop. Skimming the front page, she quickly got out the sports section. The banner headline brought a broad smile to her face.

"STEWART LEADS CLASSIC, BREAKS COURSE RECORD," it announced—not news to her eyes but ever so sweet to see confirmed in print for the ages.

Reading the details, she thought that she couldn't have been happier reading a round of her own so glowingly described. Then again, hadn't it in a sense been a round of her own? Even if she'd only imagined that she'd somehow gotten around the normal limitations of the flesh and helped Doug swing, she knew he would have been the first to give her credit for his extraordinary performance.

In fact, he had given her credit. His last words, as she'd dropped him off at his hotel, had been, "You do know, don't you, that I couldn't have done it without you?" No—those had been his next-to-last words. His last words had been so exquisitely indecent that even to remember them on a Sunday morning put her in violation of the old blue laws.

She blew a little kiss to Doug's picture on the front page, caught up on the doings of major-league baseball, and then turned to the inside pages to see how her favorite local sports columnists were calling the outcome of the Classic. Her eye was caught by another picture of Doug—not an action shot like the one on the front page but a head shot, complete with one-sided grin, of the sort that usually accompanied profiles. Sure enough, Penelope Degnan, whose byline Laurel knew from the style section and whom she'd met at parties, had done a zippy looking piece headlined "Doug Stewart: The Rabbit Is a Tiger."

Pouring herself a cup of coffee, Laurel eagerly started to read the piece. What a sly devil Doug was, not telling her it was going to appear. Was it possible that her bold lover had his shy, modest side? More likely, he'd forgotten about the profile in all the excitement of the day. Come to think of it, when had he found time to sit down with the reporter? Penelope Degnan hadn't been in Doug's gallery.

Two paragraphs into the story, the bottom fell out of Laurel's world.

"No!" she cried aloud, as she read words so scorching that she felt her eyes begin to smolder. "No!"

Groaning, pushing the paper away, burying her face in her hands, she told herself to calm down—only to find she'd forgotten the method. But why should she be calm? What difference did it make whether she smiled or screamed?

She forced herself to take a steadying sip of coffee. Then, grimly determined to drum the hideous truth into her head so she would never again be Doug Stewart's fool, she read the horrifying words again:

> "Doug Stewart is a man who loves to reconcile the unreconcilable. Born Douglas Crofton Stewart III, he says he feels more at home in the bars and cafes of Toronto's bohemian Yorkville section than in the ultrasocial Granite Club, where his parents were prominent members until their deaths last year. Primitive Eskimo art and sleek, tubular modern furniture co-exist side by side in his duplex apartment near the University of Toronto, where Stewart co-exists with movie actress Alexandra Ross and seven-year-old Jason. Does Alexandra Ross like golf? According to friends, the twenty-five-year-old actress "doesn't know a five iron from an omelette pan." Asked if this was also a comment on Ross's cooking ability, the friends said Stewart was definitely the better cook of the two. A graduate of the University of Toronto medical school, and a former staff physician at the famous "Sick Kids" Hospital in Toronto, Stewart also holds a diploma from Mae Wong's Cooking School in Toronto's Chinatown."

Numbly walking to the stove to refill her coffee cup, feeling as if she were in the midst of a nightmare, *wishing* she were in the midst of a nightmare but knowing that this was capital-*R* Reality, Laurel found one little joke to laugh at, grimly, in her anguish. She distinctly remembered that when she and Reed had gone with Elsie and Pete Howard to see a Canadian Film Board production called *Everybody Said Hello,* she had singled out the performance by a young actress named Alexandra Ross and said, "She's going places."

Alexandra Ross had gone places, all right. "Co-exists," Laurel muttered to herself, rereading the hateful article, wincing at the shabby prose. But why not shabby prose to describe a shabby relationship? She wondered if Doug had fathered seven-year-old Jason or just acquired him along with his actress and various degrees and pedigrees. Well, thank heaven for the pedigrees. When Sara delivered her inevitable I-told-you-we-shouldn't-have-let-Them-come-to-Falling-Water speech, Laurel would at least be able to point out that it had been a certified blueblood, not a member of a "certain element," who had made a fool of her.

The telephone rang. Laurel started automatically to answer it, then let her hand fall away. Was it Sara calling to gloat or Elsie calling to console or Doug calling to try to explain away his unforgivable duplicity? Hoping Dean had followed his usual pattern of turning his telephone off before he went to sleep on weekend nights, Laurel let the phone ring until the caller gave up. When the last ring had died away, she took the telephone off the hook and laid it on the table.

Lord, how shattered Dean was going to be. Laurel prayed that he wouldn't lose his faith in her and turn to Eleanor, go off with Eleanor. Though Eleanor had obviously long ago resigned herself to being a mother in name only, Laurel had no uncertainty that if Dean actually pursued her, told her she needed him, she would embrace him with open arms.

Sure. Her mind blasted open by Penelope Degnan's article, Laurel was convinced now that the truth about Eleanor lay somewhere between Elsie's perception of her and Pete's. Maybe she had been a little too interested in saving her own soul, pursuing her own artistic ambitions, when she'd left Farmingdale the first time . . . but she'd also known she was leaving her child in the hands of a loving, wise father. And maybe she'd been willing to make some sort of deal about Dean with Webb when Webb found her a New York art gallery . . . but Laurel was certain that Webb had also told her that Dean was very happy where he was, and that Laurel was as devoted as a mother could be and furthermore had just taken up with a charming golf pro who also cared about Dean.

More than happy to think about something—anything—other than Doug, Laurel pursued her train of thought. Probably Eleanor's trip to the States had been Sara's idea, not Eleanor's at all. Laurel could just imagine Sara calling Eleanor in Juan-les-Pins and saying, "You must come rescue your boy from that awful Laurel. She's taken up with a most unsuitable man." To be fair to Sara, the childless woman had probably dreaded the thought of seeing Dean taken off to Toronto. But why want him to go to France? Most likely she had counted on Laurel's affection for Dean being so strong that Eleanor's arrival would scare her into giving up all thoughts of Doug, settling down with Webb instead—and offering Dean what Sara would have imagined as an irresistible package: Farmingdale plus Webb as a stepfather.

When Webb had learned the depth of Laurel's feeling for Doug, and been personally charmed by Doug over drinks, he had persuaded Sara that the Eleanor caper wasn't in Dean's best interests, after all, and was doomed to failure. So they'd made the trip worthwhile by throwing in the gallery angle, and Eleanor had agreed to do what she'd all along seen as the better part of wisdom— letting others love Dean day to day while she loved him at a distance.

Well, there was one puzzle solved, Laurel thought, her eyes straying back to Penelope Degnan's profile of the low-life, duplicitous, utterly heartbreaking Douglas Crofton Stewart III—doctor, chef, golfer, and international rat. Why had he done it? Weren't there enough kicks in his life without his having to be the man of a thousand masks? Damn him to hell, Laurel thought miserably, the hot tears coursing down her face. If there was any justice on this earth, Doug Stewart would double-bogie every hole out there at Falling Water today.

She wiped her eyes, went upstairs, took a quick shower, and put on jeans, a plaid shirt, and sneakers. Wishing she could somehow shield Dean from the truth, but knowing she could at best buy him an hour of blissful ignorance, she left the article on the kitchen table, along with a note asking him to meet her at the Rainbow Pool down on Fisherman's Way. She started toward the back door, then turned around and squeezed a large glassful of orange juice for Dean. This was no morning for him to have to squeeze his own juice, poor baby.

Putting the top down on the Mercedes, she tried to find pleasure in the warm sun on her face, the teasing wind in her hair. But her mind had a mind of its own today, and insisted on remembering other sorts of pleasures she'd shared with Doug.

She turned the radio on and found that every station was playing a song that seemed to be about her and Doug. She switched to a news station, only to wonder how Doug felt about the space shuttle that had just been launched, and what he made of the unrest in the Middle East.

She reminded herself to tell Dean that she thought Sara and Evan ought to be encouraged to get involved with Inner City Youth. Once the Camp ICY season was over, perhaps they could be persuaded to sponsor a special program at Falling Water for golf-mad kids like John Coover. Maybe if Dean offered to work with them, they would even turn their spacious house into a dormitory on those weekends. Having kids around the house would probably perform miracles for Sara's disposition—and might even be an inspiration for Ev to cut down on his drinking. The idea of the program really warmed Laurel, but hardly distracted her from the agony at hand. How

could she think about John Coover and about golf and
not think about Doug?

How could she think about anything and not think
about Doug?

As she turned off Farmingdale River Road onto Fishermen's Way, she realized that Doug was teeing off just
about now. For one malicious moment, she wondered
about trying to think herself into his club but *away* from
the sweet spot—but even if such a ridiculous thing were
possible, she knew she wouldn't do it. She knew one
thing for absolutely sure about Doug Stewart, and it was
that he was a man of exceptional physical grace, a natural
golfer of a caliber she'd never seen before and didn't
expect ever to see again. Despite the part of her mind
that thought he deserved to shoot a disastrous round,
another part hoped, very simply, that he would win.

She pulled her car off the road near the bend in the
Farmingdale River known as Rainbow Pool. She made
her way down toward the river, sliding on fallen leaves,
kicking stones, stepping on twigs, and filling the woods
with the crackling sounds beloved of children. When she
got down to the water's edge, she found herself a rock
to sit on, and—as silent and motionless as if someone
were about to putt—she watched for the widening ripples
that would tell her that a trout was feeding on something
beneath the surface.

After a while she took off her sneakers and socks and
stuck her feet in the water just to know what if felt like.
It felt cold. She couldn't remember the last time that
she'd indulged in a simple act of childlike curiosity.
Sticking your feet in water wasn't an activity at which
one could be a champion, after all.

Half wishing she'd brought a book with her, half glad
she hadn't, she checked out the varying shades of moss
and lichen growing around the proud old trees that shaded
the river; she walked a hundred feet upstream to a curious
meadowlike patch of bank where she counted eleven

different kinds of wildflowers, ranging from simple buttercups to a purple bell-shaped flower intricately streaked with pink and white. Several times she thought she heard a car coming, only to realize it was the sound of the water, which mysteriously seemed to change pitch now and then—maybe because of the wind?

And she thought about Doug. Willed herself not to, but found that her will was as fragile as a wildflower. She toyed with the idea of finding a bottle somewhere, and writing a note on a piece of paper from the pad she kept in her glove department, and setting it adrift downstream. With a little luck it would drift into the nameless brook that flowed under the Epstein farm and surfaced as the famous water hazard on the twelfth hole at the club.

What would she write?

I hate you. I love you.

Because the balance of warm sun and river breeze was lulling her body into a somnolent state, and because she wanted to get away from the thoughts she was no longer remotely able to control, she got an old plaid blanket from the trunk of her car, stretched it out in the meadow full of wildflowers—being careful not to crush any of the lovely blooms—and lay down to sleep.

Confusion pursued her across the border into the land of nod. She loved him. She hated him. He was a buck deer bounding through the woods in a state of grace, and he was a vile, horned beast trampling through the sand traps of life and refusing to rake his footprints. He was an old friend she had known many lives ago, when she liked to go fishing with her uncle, and he was the ultimately unknowable stranger who would turn red just when you thought you had the green go-ahead signal. He was John Coover's father, Dean's father, her father . . . and he was a snarling watchdog owned by a boy named Jason who led him around on a leash handmade by Ben Hogan. He was familiar, strange; good, bad; challenging, easy; he was all the men she needed rolled into one.

He was—

—good Lord. Such an extraordinarily convincing dream: the hair glinting gold in the sunlight; the hazel eyes flecked with the green of the meadow; the mouth angry—no, loving—no, angry *and* loving.

And not a dream at all.

Doug Stewart was there.

"What are you doing here?" Laurel stammered, gracelessly.

"Looking for a lost ball," Doug said. "It's small, round, and orange, with a dimpled surface and two dots on the—"

"Seriously, Doug! Why aren't you on the course?"

Dropping down casually to sit on a corner of her blanket, he said, "Because Dean did what you should have done, you absurd, untrusting, headstrong person. He went to an instrument known as the telephone, and he called me."

"Called you?" Laurel echoed.

"Sure. You know. Take the receiver off the hook, and then you put your finger in the little—"

"Doug, stop it! You have no right to—"

"No right to what? No right to expect trust from the woman who claims to love me? Trust in me, and trust in her perceptions of me, instead of trust in a blithering piece of newspaper drivel?"

"Sorry, Doug," Laurel said coldly, "you'll have to do better than that. The *Courant* is a respectable paper, and—"

"And I'm a golf bum and not to be believed? I'm not saying there wasn't a shred of truth in the story," Doug said. "That's just about how much truth there was—a shred. I *do* like Eskimo art. If I ever meet that short-story writer who masquerades as a reporter, I think I'll use her as a target on the driving range." Fixing his hazel eyes on Laurel, his mouth twisting in anger, he said, "But you're the one I'm really sore at. Your bright little mind leaped to put the worst possible interpretation on every so-called fact in that story, eh? I don't suppose it occurred to you that Alexandra Ross might be my sister?"

"Your sister?" Laurel echoed incredulously.

"As a matter of fact, she's not my sister," Doug said. "But why didn't you at least consider that possibility? The truth happens to be just about as innocent. Her family and mine lived next door to each other. I used to baby-sit for her, and we never lost touch. She married and had a baby too damn young, and when the marriage broke up I was the person she came running to. I was going through a spot of trouble myself at the time, and we decided to share an apartment. Separate bedrooms, darling Laurel. Ms. Penelope Degnan no doubt fully intended to add a bit of spice to the breakfasts of the good citizens of greater Hartford today, but 'co-exist' is not necessarily a euphemism for 'shack up.' I could no more make love to Alexandra than I could to a sister."

"Oh," Laurel said, her voice neutral. "What was the spot of trouble you were having?"

"I was in love with a damn fool woman who wouldn't leave her husband even though she didn't love him—only loved his money. She was perfectly willing to have an affair with me, only I didn't go for that idea. There was a lot of tension for a while, until I came to my senses."

Picking up a pebble and sending it skipping downstream, Laurel said, "What if she left her husband now? Would you—"

"She did leave him. When my money situation changed. Her timing opened my eyes in a hurry. You see, my parents cut me off when I turned my back on medicine. My father was a doctor, and it didn't matter to him that I was hooked on golf at age five—golf was for Sundays, and I damn well was going to be a doctor like him and his father before him. I gave it a try—I was a researcher, not a pediatrician, by the way, though Sick Kids is a great hospital and I would have been proud to work there—and then, after a few miserable years, I said the hell with it. I got myself a job as a teaching pro—and the rest is history. My parents did in their wills what they were too proud to do in life—admitted that they'd been wrong in trying to mold me, declaring that a son was a son even if he was a jock." He laughed.

"What?" Laurel said.

"If only they'd encouraged me to turn pro when I was a kid, they would have saved us all a lot of grief. I'm glad I joined the tour, mostly because it brought me to you. And it's been one hell of an exciting time, in that special way things are exciting when they're old dreams you'd begun to believe you would never get to live out. But I can't make a life of this. I realized that last night. I was in the wrong branch of medicine for me, but I can't turn my back on all that training. There's a new specialty of sports medicine, and I'm thinking about getting into that. I'll be competing for places with younger doctors, but I guess I've proved I'm a pretty good midlife rabbit, eh?"

"Oh, Doug," Laurel said, not knowing where to look, then meeting his hazel eyes straight on. "I suppose I ought to be thoroughly ashamed of myself. But, damn it, if only you'd told me everything from the beginning—"

Doug took her hands in his. Around them bird songs rose and fell, and the water in the river changed pitch again. "My life has been one long series of people loving me conditionally. My parents loving me—if I went into medicine. Then the woman who wanted me—when I inherited the money. I wanted to know that you cared about me even thinking that I was a jock, with a chancy income, and not much in the way of social credentials. The middle name is Crampton, by the way, not Crofton.

And I'm afraid I'm not Douglas Crampton Stewart the Third. I'm the one and only. The first, anyway. I always thought a junior might be a nice thing to have around someday." Tucking fingers under Laurel's chin, he added softly, "Or a little Miss Blue. Do you think Dean would be awfully embarrassed if we started having babies?"

"You don't think we're past it?" Laurel murmured.

"At thirty-two and thirty-seven? Hell, no. Like I said, Lady Blue, I'm a great midlife rabbit. And I happen to love you. A lot."

"Oh, Lord, Doug, I love you so much, I don't know which way is up."

Doug solemnly pointed toward the ground.

"I still can't believe you care enough about me to walk out on the Classic and disqualify yourself," Laurel marveled.

"I still can't believe you care enough about me so that you had to run off into the woods."

"What do you mean?" Laurel asked.

"Would our old friend Lady Blue have run off because she read something in a newspaper that upset her? Hell, no. She would have swallowed her upsetness along with her morning orange juice, put on a mask along with her hairband, and let everyone at Falling Water know how good she was at rising above it. Tell me if I'm wrong, darling, but I don't think you worried about how the world at large would read that article. You thought about you and me. About you and Dean and me."

"I wasn't too thrilled thinking about Sara reading it. In fact, I took the phone off the hook mostly because I didn't want her to reach me."

"Exactly!" Doug said. "Thereby signaling to her or anyone else who tried to get you that you cared. Were upset. Were hurt. Cool, collected Lady Blue Laurel Campion never took the telephone off the hook. Disaster would strike, and she'd just carry right on, business as usual, because it was her head that ruled her, not her heart. Heads are wonderful, darling, and heaven knows I value yours—but they can get in the way."

"Loose impediments," Laurel murmured.

"Artificial obstructions," Doug laughed. "Have you ever made love in a meadow?"

Much later, at the awards banquet, Evan Campion asked, "Laurel, will you be insulted if I toast you in ginger ale?"

"Seeing you drink ginger ale makes me so happy, I might just cry," Laurel answered.

"Again?" Sara said, a smile on her face. "You're a one-woman water hazard tonight. Actually, I may cry myself," she whispered, as the two women leaned across the table to hug.

"I do love all this mushy stuff," Clare Hamilton sighed.

Pete Howard blew his nose. "I say we all just have rose fever."

Laying her cheek against his shoulder, Elsie said, "Such a romantic, darling. Laurel, are you sure you want to marry a doctor?"

"She's sure," Dean declared, his eyes sparkling.

"Lawyers are really much easier to get along with," Webb Daniels said to Clare.

An expectant hush fell over the Falling Water dining room as the president of the club ascended to the podium and tapped on the microphone.

"I remember that man," Eleanor Campion Ligeret said. "He always did want to be president of something. I suppose he'll make a very long speech. But it's nice when people get what they want, isn't it?"

"And want what they get," Doug murmured into Laurel's ear. "And want, and want, and want, my Laurel-Laurie—"

Clearing his throat, Evan said, "I better get this in before they start handing out the checks. I must say I'm glad that if it couldn't be Doug collecting the big honors, it's that nice boy from Wampannoag." He raised his glass of ginger ale, winking at Doug. "To Laurel," Evan said, "whose last name will no longer rhyme with champion— but still sounds like a winner to me."

Second Chance at Love

Second Chance at Love

All of the above titles are $1.75 per copy

___ 05625-1 **MOURNING BRIDE #57** Lucia Curzon
___ 06411-4 **THE GOLDEN TOUCH #58** Robin James
___ 06596-X **EMBRACED BY DESTINY #59** Simone Hadary
___ 06660-5 **TORN ASUNDER #60** Ann Cristy
___ 06573-0 **MIRAGE #61** Margie Michaels
___ 06650-8 **ON WINGS OF MAGIC #62** Susanna Collins
___ 05816-5 **DOUBLE DECEPTION #63** Amanda Troy
___ 06675-3 **APOLLO'S DREAM #64** Claire Evans
___ 06676-1 **SMOLDERING EMBERS #65** Marie Charles
___ 06677-X **STORMY PASSAGE #66** Laurel Blake
___ 06678-8 **HALFWAY THERE #67** Aimée Duvall
___ 06679-6 **SURPRISE ENDING #68** Elinor Stanton
___ 06680-X **THE ROGUE'S LADY #69** Anne Devon
___ 06681-8 **A FLAME TOO FIERCE #70** Jan Mathews
___ 06682-6 **SATIN AND STEELE #71** Jaelyn Conlee
___ 06683-4 **MIXED DOUBLES #72** Meredith Kingston
___ 06684-2 **RETURN ENGAGEMENT #73** Kay Robbins
___ 06685-0 **SULTRY NIGHTS #74** Ariel Tierney
___ 06686-9 **AN IMPROPER BETROTHMENT #75** Henrietta Houston
___ 06687-7 **FORSAKING ALL OTHERS #76** LaVyrle Spencer
___ 06688-5 **BEYOND PRIDE #77** Kathleen Ash
___ 06689-3 **SWEETER THAN WINE #78** Jena Hunt
___ 06690-7 **SAVAGE EDEN #79** Diane Crawford
___ 06691-5 **STORMY REUNION #80** Jasmine Craig
___ 06692-3 **THE WAYWARD WIDOW #81** Anne Mayfield
___ 06693-1 **TARNISHED RAINBOW #82** Jocelyn Day
___ 06694-X **STARLIT SEDUCTION #83** Anne Reed
___ 06695-8 **LOVER IN BLUE #84** Aimée Duvall
___ 06696-6 **THE FAMILIAR TOUCH #85** Lynn Lawrence
___ 06697-4 **TWILIGHT EMBRACE #86** Jennifer Rose
___ 06698-2 **QUEEN OF HEARTS #87** Lucia Curzon

All of the above titles are $175 per copy

WHAT READERS SAY ABOUT
SECOND CHANCE AT LOVE BOOKS

"Your books are the greatest!"
—*M. N., Carteret, New Jersey**

"I have been reading romance novels for quite some time, but the SECOND CHANCE AT LOVE books are the most enjoyable."
—*P. R., Vicksburg, Mississippi**

"I enjoy SECOND CHANCE [AT LOVE] more than any books that I have read and I do read a lot."
—*J. R., Gretna, Louisiana**

"For years I've had my subscription in to Harlequin. Currently there is a series called Circle of Love, but you have them all beat."
—*C. B., Chicago, Illinois**

"I really think your books are exceptional . . . I read Harlequin and Silhouette and although I still like them, I'll buy your books over theirs. SECOND CHANCE [AT LOVE] is more interesting and holds your attention and imagination with a better story line . . ."
—*J. W., Flagstaff, Arizona**

"I've read many romances, but yours take the 'cake'!"
—*D. H., Bloomsburg, Pennsylvania**

"Have waited ten years for *good* romance books. Now I have them."
—*M. P., Jacksonville, Florida**

*Names and addresses available upon request